PRINCE, SLAVE, SOLDIER, KING

*Tom Peters, a life
that mattered*

After the American War of Independence (1775–83), Tom Peters became the leader of the British Army's Black Pioneers and other former slaves who were evacuated to Nova Scotia. In this story the main events of his life from enslavement up until his trial in Sierra Leone, are fact-based: how he came to be enslaved and how he escaped; how he enlisted in the British Army and as a natural leader was promoted, becoming a spokesman for the Africans; how he travelled to London in 1791 and addressed the House of Commons in the cause of emancipation and settling the colony of Sierra Leone under the auspices of the Sierra Leone Company. Widely regarded as the founding father of the colony, but regarded by the Governor as a rival to his authority, Tom Peters was forced to stand trial and was convicted of theft on unreliable evidence. He died of fever shortly afterwards. His associations with historical figures in the story are all thought to be true, but other characters and all the conversations, family chronology, his childhood and his death, are imagined.

PRINCE, SLAVE, SOLDIER, KING

Tom Peters, a life that mattered

Victoria Eyre

with illustrations by
Sofie Baker
and Theo Dingwall-Main

Unicorn Press

For Patrick

First published in Great Britain in 2021 by Unicorn Press
60 Bracondale
Norwich
NR1 2BE

tradfordhugh@gmail.com
www.unicornpublishing.org

Text Copyright © 2021 Victoria Eyre
Illustrations Copyright © 2021 Sofie Baker and Theo Dingwall-Main
Page 98: General Sir Henry Clinton, mons.wikipedia.org/w/index.php?curid=13353817
Jacket front illustration: Statue of Thomas Peters erected in 2011, in Freetown, Sierra Leone
    by the Krio Descendants Union. Photograph Copyright © Meserette Kentake

All rights reserved. Without limiting the rights under copyright reserved above, no part
of this publication may be reproduced, stored or introduced into a retrieval system, or
transmitted, in any form or by any means (electronic, mechanical, photocopying, recording
or otherwise), without the prior written permission of both the copyright owner and the
publisher of this book.

A CIP record of this book can be obtained from the British Library

ISBN 978 1 838395 30 8

Acknowledgements
My thanks to Gillian Graham Dobson for her outstanding editing and advice.
Thanks also to Nicola Graham and to the Reverend Alison Levesley for their insights.

Design by newtonworks.uk
Printed in the UK by Swallowtail Print, Norwich

CONTENTS

PRINCE

'Go on in the name of God, in the name of His might, till even American slavery, the vilest that ever saw the sun, shall vanish away before it.'

John Wesley to William Wilberforce
(possibly the last letter he ever wrote)

The man hurried into the room carrying a child. His wife lay on the bed, her face glistening with the fever. A girl stood fanning her. The man put the child down and took the young girl to the door.

'Quickly,' he said, 'run to your mother. Go now, and thank you.'

The girl ran. The man turned back and said to his wife, 'The drums are speaking, you must hide.' The woman knew what he meant. The slavers were coming. They had bribed a neighbouring kingdom to invade her husband's kingdom. After fighting, both sides would be exhausted and easy to capture.

'You must hide,' he said it again.

He unlocked a heavy wooden chest from the wall and pushed it aside. The chest covered a secret opening into a cave. He lifted his wife gently and carried her through the opening. Their little son followed, holding the hem of his father's robe. The robe identified his father as a king. He wore it only for ceremonial occasions or when, as he had just done, he spoke to his people. Light streamed through a gap in the rock face. It was the only other way into the cave, and it was protected from prying eyes by a bush. The cave was above a pathway which the slavers would use. The mother and child's safety was dependent on the child's not making too much noise. The man had put food and water in the cave earlier in the day. He lowered his wife on to the bed and, taking a cup, filled it from a gourd.

'Drink, dearest.' He held it to her lips. The whites of her eyes were blood-shot. Her fever was dangerously high. Would she live? He did not know. He had to go. The child looked at his father expectantly. He was excited and wanted to go with him. The man held his finger to his lips, to tell the child that he must be good and quiet. He poured him a drink of goats' milk and gave him a banana. He was the King. His people needed him. He hated leaving his wife and child by themselves.

'I must go now. Look after your mother and be a man.' The child's face fell. He stared at his father, worried and disappointed. The man smiled down at him. 'We will have an adventure. I will come later.' The child smiled.

Gravely ill, his mother lay on the bed, barely conscious. The little boy ate his banana and snuggled up to her. She put her arm around him. He fell asleep. Hours later he awoke. He could hear a noise, shouting and clanking.

'Babba,' (father) he said.

His mother did not stir. Her arm was still tight around him. Her body was cold and clammy. Something was wrong. He must find his father. He struggled to get out of the tightened arm, then, kissing her damp face, he whispered again, 'Babba, fetch Babba,' and crawled towards the light. Outside the cave, he found himself under the bush and looking down through the leaves, he saw people passing by. Some had iron collars and others had wooden collars around their necks. Chains attached them to each other. They were shuffling along the path. Behind the men, the women were chained in pairs. He did not understand what was happening, but he would go down. He felt sure that one of them would take him to his father. The hill was steep and rocky. He was nearly down, when he lost his balance and rolled into a ditch. Cut, scratched and scared, his courage deserted him. He shouted as loudly as he could, 'BAABAAA!' and he began to sob. The clanking noise stopped, the feet stopped shuffling and a man lifted him out of the ditch. It was not his father. The people stood still. They looked dejected. The man holding the child stood in front of them. A murmur ran through the captives, 'The King's son.'

A young girl screamed and fell to her knees, dragging her companion with her.

'You know this child?' asked the man.

'Little prince. Nursey-girl,' she pointed to herself.

'Your King is dead,' said the man, but compassion touched his heart. He was a father too, besides which, the child was good-looking and might fetch some money.

'You be his mamma-woman. You take him.'

The collars were taken from the girl's neck and replaced with chains around her waist. Weeping, she took the child. Soon they moved on, the child riding in a cloth sling on her back. He knew her. The previous day, he had been playing with her, but why was she sad and where was she taking him? Confusion and anguish overcame him. When would he see his father? Should he have left his mother? He was barely three years old and had lost both his parents. In a state of profound shock, he passed out, whimpering in semi-consciousness.

◄◄ 2 ►►

Day after day, they trudged through the forest, down the dusty sun-dappled path. Colobus monkeys leapt through the treetops and parrots screeched their warnings. The leading slaver banged on a metal plate with a big ladle. The sound combined with the clanking chains to scare wild animals. They retreated deeper into the forest, leaving the path clear for snakes, insects and baboons, all of them, as ever, undaunted by human presence. Elephants could be heard crashing through the bushes a little way off. Meeting them on the path with a gang of chained slaves who could not escape, might be a disaster.

On the fifth day of their captivity, they came out of the forest and trudged under some giant baobab trees before coming to a track which took them past an impressively large fort. The fort was on the Ashanti coast overlooking the Atlantic Ocean. It was built of stone, painted white and had several courtyards. It looked impregnable. After a few hundred yards, the slaves, thirsty, footsore and miserable, stopped by the high walls which surrounded the barracoons.

Pedro, a Portuguese, employed by his government to manage the fort, was waiting by the barracoons to count the slaves. He walked down the line and had just finished, when a fishing boat tied up at the moorings and two men were helped out. 'Oh good, Father Thierry,' said Pedro. 'Good morning Father, thank you for coming. There are thirty men, eight women and a child.' Father Thierry, the French Roman Catholic priest, who ministered to four separate slave posts along a stretch of the Ashanti coast, had come to baptise the slaves.

◄◄ **3** ►►

The first time Pedro had set eyes on his wife, she had been at the end of an identical line of slaves – tall, black and beautiful. Her sorrowful face had touched his heart, and, on the spur of the moment, he had intervened to prevent her from being loaded on to the ship.

'I need more house servants. I'll take the two at the end.' He had turned away as if 'the two at the end' were simply a matter of convenience. The young women had been unchained and taken to the fort. For weeks Pedro had been overcome by guilt. The girls had had each other for company, but they had lost their families, their homes, their futures and their pasts. He had hated seeing such misery. He had hated causing such misery, and he still hated it.

Pedro had comforted himself that the girls' lives would have been far worse had they boarded that vessel. Something in him had changed. With every new intake of slaves, he had begun to feel increasingly disturbed. As a devout Christian, he thanked God for the sacrament of Holy Baptism through which their souls had been saved. It gave him a feeling of deep spiritual satisfaction. Nevertheless, he had been troubled. The beautiful girl's sorrowful face had haunted his dreams. The sacrament of Holy Baptism was paramount – but, even so, Enslavement? Transportation? – Could they ever be justified?

Three months later, the beautiful girl and her friend had looked happier. Pedro had fallen deeply in love and, more than anything, he had wanted to marry her. She had been baptised when she arrived at the fort, and in the first three months, she had learnt to speak Portuguese and Coastal Akan. Whenever he had seen her and her friend, he had stopped to ask after their health and then he had quickly moved away. One day, she had been alone. On an impulse, he had said, 'Will you marry me?'

She had looked at him and had replied quietly, 'You seem to be a good man. I will marry you.'

Pedro had been overjoyed. Father Thierry had married them. His clerk had been Pedro's best man and Miriam, his wife's friend, had been her brides-maid. Within a year, a son, Carlos, had been born. They both loved that child more than anything in the world.

Pedro prayed for the slaves, and for his wife and child, while the new slaves were being baptised. He still loved his wife just as much as he always had. He had given her everything she wanted, and more besides. A Moroccan trader from Rabat dispatched fine materials by ship. They included Chinese silks that had come from Alexandria. He delighted in seeing her dressed in beautifully-coloured clothes, jewellery and headdresses.

The servants called her 'Nora', their version of 'Senhora'. They loved her and would do anything for her. They knew of nowhere else on the Ashanti coast where they would be as safe and well-cared-for as they were in the Pedro fort. They wanted it to stay that way. To leave the fort was to risk abduction, and transportation by a more vicious slaver. The Senhora's women friends were her servants. There were eight women house servants, ten men servants, and twelve guards. All the men, whatever their employment, had been trained to use a musket.

◄◄ **4** ►►

Father Thierry and his server had come to the end of the line. He was baptis-ing the last two slaves, a little boy and a teenage girl. The child put his hand out to touch the priest's stole as he lent over him. Pedro looked again at the child. He had an idea. Carlos, his son, needed a playmate. He was being diffi-cult. He would scream if he did not get his own way, and never, ever, did what he was told, without making a fuss. Pedro and the Senhora had agreed that they should find a companion for him. Pedro signalled to a slaver:

'Those two, take them in.'

The slaver released the teenage girl from her waist chain. Terrified and fearing for their lives, she gathered the child to her. Then, with her arm gripped by the slaver, and followed by Pedro and his servant, they went through the gates and into the fort.

In the courtyard, Pedro spoke to his servant:

'Fetch the Senhora. Please.'

The servant hurried off. A few minutes later the Senhora came into the courtyard. Everyone bowed, except for the teenage girl, who fell to her knees as she had been accustomed to doing to the child's parents.

The Senhora looked at the girl and the child. The child stared back in wonderment, for, to him, the Senhora was a vision of loveliness. She wore beautifully coloured clothes and a head dress which shone with pretty stones. The child was entranced. The Senhora crossed the courtyard and bent down to look at him. The child laughed, his eyes shining with excitement as he reached up to her beautiful face.

'Shall we keep him?' Pedro asked. 'He looks healthy.'

'Let's see, husband. Please will you fetch Carlos.'

Pedro left the courtyard to return a few moments later holding a pale brown boy by the hand.

'Carlos, this is your friend,' Pedro spoke in Portuguese. The pale brown boy laughed. He ran up to the child and punched him in the stomach. The rough-looking slaver took the teenage girl by the arm and started to pull her towards the gate. She screamed. The child had heard her scream before. Now, with wounded feelings and hurting stomach, faint memories flickered in his mind. With a cry he ran to her, clasped her leg and vomited.

The Senhora was not pleased. She clapped her hands. 'Husband, quick, stop him. Leave her alone. She stays. The little one needs her.'

'Of course, my dear, of course, I am so sorry.' Pedro turned and spoke to the slaver. The slaver nodded, dropped the girl's arm, and left.

◄◄ 5 ►►

The Senhora gave orders and her servants hurried around preparing a room in the women's courtyard. The girl and the child would live there. They were given beds and a stool. Two young women, a little older than the girl, brought a basin half filled with water and a drying cloth. They smiled and signalled that the child should be washed. Another servant brought drinking water, fruit and coconut slices.

The child laughed as he sat in the basin, splashing the water, and when the girl had washed and dried him, she sat him on the stool with a coconut slice while she washed herself.

The room was small and dark. It had an earth floor and a mahogany-wood door that was slightly too short, but no window. A family of geckos lurked near the gap above the door, lying in wait for unsuspecting mosquitoes. Miriam brought the girl some cloth and showed her how to wind it around her body. She cut two extra lengths to cover her and the child at night to protect them from the mosquitoes that had avoided the geckos. She smiled and spoke kindly to the girl. The girl could not understand but she smiled back.

'The staff', as the Senhora called them, were cared for and treated more as family than as servants. Royal by birth, she was aware of the debilitating depression that enslavement could cause. Enslavement, as a proud and haughty princess, had been particularly humiliating, but the Senhora was clever, kind and pragmatic. Her beauty and kindness had brought her a good husband, and she had formed a happy and contented environment for those who lived in the fort.

The fort had been adapted according to her wishes. She had been determined that Carlos, their child, should not be affected by the atmosphere of misery and fear which engulfed it when slaves were imprisoned in the lower ground barracoon. New barracoons had been built further down the coast and the barracoon beneath the fort had been white-washed and converted into rooms for the guards and for the nightwatchmen. Pedro had asked Father Thierry to purify the new rooms with holy water before he would allow the men servants to move in.

The Senhora spoke to the servants in Portuguese, telling them that anyone who upset the girl or the child would be sent to the barracoons.

They all understood that this was the Senhora's way of saying that something was important to her. They knew how much she valued them, and they knew that she had no intention of sending any of them anywhere at all – let alone, to the barracoons. In fact, the only person who had ever been sent to the barracoons had been a witch doctor who had been threatening the women servants.

◂ ◂ 6 ▸ ▸

The girl was to look after the child. She already loved him with all her heart, and the child loved her back – every bit as much as she loved him.

Trauma had changed their lives, and obliterated the child's memories. He could remember neither his parents nor his home. Some nights he would wake from a dream sobbing. He didn't know why. The girl stroked his head. She spoke to him in his tribal language and called him by his tribal name. She told him that it was only a dream.

The child had been given the baptismal name of Tomas. Carlos, called him 'Tom' and, before long, they were the best of friends. The only time they were allowed outside the fort was for two hours in the morning when, accompanied by two minders, two armed guards, Miriam and the girl, they were taken down to the sea, and taught to swim. After swimming, they played on the beach, building forts and tunnels in the sand. They did not like the crabs and were terrified of the iguanas who appeared from nowhere to wander aimlessly across the sand. If the sea was too rough the little boys would go, instead, into the men's courtyard which was unoccupied in the daytime. There, the minders would play games with them or teach them to hop, jump, skip, catch and throw.

In the evenings they were allowed into the Senhora's private courtyard. It was a smaller courtyard in which she had created a garden. Orange trees had been brought from Portugal. Purple bougainvillea grew against the walls, and the smell of frangipani permeated the air. A bronze statue of a soldier stood against one wall. It had come from the Kingdom of Benin and was the Senhora's most prized possession. The children enjoyed standing beside it, pretending that they, too. were soldiers. In the courtyard, Pedro would play with them, and the Senhora would tell them stories and feed them coconut slices, cashew nuts and orange juice.

Before they went to bed, the boys went with Pedro into his chapel. A table covered with a white cloth stood against the far wall. A cross had been placed on top, and, in front of it, lay a bible. The boys knelt beside Pedro while he said the Lord's Prayer in Latin. They learnt it by heart and knew that it was holy and important, but they did not understand the words. Pedro was content. That they knew it by heart was, for him, enough.

After chapel, Pedro would leave to do his evening rounds. The boys stayed with the Senhora. She would hold them together on her lap and sing them the songs of her childhood. Gradually, they relaxed and grew sleepy. When Tom's mamma-woman and Miriam came to collect them, they were almost asleep and had to be carried to their beds.

The Senhora had a soft spot for Tom. She believed him, as she was herself, to be of royal descent. He amused her with his broad smile. He would clap and hop up and down with excitement whenever he saw her in her beautiful clothes and jewellery. Both she and Pedro were delighted with the change in Carlos. Their little boy was so much happier now that he had a friend, and, under the influence of this strange child, he was behaving himself very much better. She accepted Tom as a second son, but, understanding how important his mamma-woman was to him, she made sure that she, too, was protected and cared for.

Sometimes when they were on the beach the children would see a ship. The ship was beautiful to watch, with its sails billowing out in front of it. It was on its way to pick up slaves from further down the coast. The children knew nothing of the misery and anguish of the cargo which would be concealed beneath the elegance of its sails, as it turned away from Africa to sail the Atlantic Ocean.

As well as the slave ships, at least twice a month a cargo ship would drop anchor outside the fort to unload orders for the kingdoms. The sea in front of the fort was unusually deep, which meant that ships could anchor closer to the shore than at many other ports. For that reason, it had become the favoured drop-off point for some cargo ships. It was cheaper and more convenient than the main ports. Men and their camels would wait behind the fort to collect and transport the goods, either to the Ashanti capital, Kumasi, or to neighbouring kingdoms.

None of the European governments would ever have considered sending a married man to manage a slave post. Pedro had arrived at the fort, a bachelor, and he had married a slave. Now, with two growing and increasingly energetic boys, he and his wife had a problem. There were no schools on the coast, and the boys needed far more exercise than it was possible to give them in two hours on the beach. The Senhora talked to Miriam, 'What are we going to do, Miriam? They can't sit still for a single second.' Miriam laughed. 'That's boys for you, Nora. Why don't you allow them into the men's courtyard in the evenings? They are old enough, and they would enjoy the dancing.'

The men servants and the women servants lived in separate courtyards. Other than those who were on duty, they would congregate every evening in the men's courtyard for their leisure time of singing, dancing, playing the drums, telling and re-telling tribal legends.

After leaving the Senhora's courtyard the next day, the boys were taken into the men's courtyard. The drums were brought out and the dancing began. The rhythms would change, then change again. Every change and every rhythm had a different meaning. They learnt to understand which rhythms asked questions, and which gave answers. As with the drums, so it was with African dance – it had a language of its own. The boys danced until they were tired out and, as Miriam had predicted, they enjoyed every minute of it. From then on, it became their nightly routine.

The boys thought of everyone at the fort as part of their extended family. They grew up with their own minders, their own guards and their own carers. Everyone they knew was always there, ready to help, support or comfort them. Their lives were happy and untroubled. They were so carefully shielded, that, at twelve years old, they were only peripherally aware of the slave trade. It was at that age they began to realize that the intermittent commotion outside the fort, was connected to Pedro, to the fort and, usually, to a ship moored in the bay. The noise would stop as the ship turned to sail over the horizon. The boys were nearly old enough to be allowed on to the battlements by themselves and, from there, the Senhora realised, they would see the slaves being taken from the barracoons and forced on to the ship. She and Pedro decided that they should be sent out on 'Adventure' days when the slaves were being loaded. Pedro made arrangements for their minders, and two armed guards, to take them out early, and not to return with them until late. The boys were delighted at the thought of so much freedom. Their minders taught them to shoot with a bow and arrow, to throw a spear, and to track wild animals. They were allowed to explore, to climb trees and rocks, and to swim on the reef. On their return to the fort, they would run up to the battlements as the sky was turning red. From there, they watched the ship sail over the horizon, a black silhouette against the setting sun.

◂ ◂ 8 ▸ ▸

One dark night, the men and boys were dancing and the drums were playing when sudden gunfire shattered the peace. The noise sent Pedro running up to the battlements. 'What is it? What did you see?'

The nightwatchman answered, 'Three men, I think, Sir. I saw their shadows, but they have put something down by the gates.'

Peering over the battlements, they could make out the shape of a man.

'Come on, let's go!' They ran down the stairs.

Pedro said, 'When I open the gate, fire a shot in case it's a trick. Ready?'

'Yes, sir, ready, sir.' The nightwatchman fired a shot into the air.

The man lying outside the gate was still alive. He was an elderly African. He wore an unusual embroidered garment which marked him out as foreign to the coastal area, and probably someone of importance. He was carried into the men's courtyard where he was given a room and, there, he was cared for and nursed back to health.

His name was Ibrahim. When he regained his health, he told Pedro that he had been captured by rebels, who had tried to overthrow the Malian government. He had been with the Mansa of Mali and his entourage on their way back from a state visit to Ashanti when they were ambushed outside Kumasi. In the ensuing fracas, the rebels had mistakenly abducted Ibrahim instead of the Mansa. Knowing that the Assantehene, the Ashanti Emperor, would immediately send troops to cut them off to the North, the rebels had turned South towards the coastal region taking Ibrahim with them. There Ibrahim, who was not a young man, had succumbed to the trauma and had lost consciousness. Having to carry Ibrahim and, having unexpectedly, encountered an army patrol operating along the coast, the rebels panicked. They dumped Ibrahim, stole a boat and escaped by sea.

For twenty years, Ibrahim had been a professor at Sankore University near Timbuktu, one of the oldest universities in the world. He could speak several languages including Portuguese and basic English. He could write Arabic and the Latin alphabet, and he had studied the Vai, Adinkra and Nsibidi scripts. He was an astronomer, a philosopher, a mathematician and an expert on early African antiquities. He would only, ever, leave the university, if he was required to accompany the Mansa on state occasions. Soon after his recovery, a deputation had arrived from rhe Assantehene to ask that Ibrahim be returned to the Palace at Kumasi. They left when Pedro told them that he was still too poorly to survive such a long journey.

Surprisingly, Ibrahim seemed to be quite content with his new home. Pedro felt that there must be much more that he had not been told, but he liked Ibrahim. Pedro had a rosary and Ibrahim had prayer beads. They were of different faiths, but the beads linked them in a relationship of mutual trust. He was respectful and gentle but, for religious reasons, the evening entertainment made him uneasy. After he had recovered, he had been moved out of the men's courtyard and given a lower-ground room next to the guards.

◂◂ 9 ▸▸

It was the Senhora's suggestion to ask Ibrahim if he would consider educating the boys. Knowing that he was still alive, only due to the kindness and care that he had been given, Ibrahim was glad to have a way of repaying those to whom he owed his life. He missed teaching, and he liked the boys. He agreed immediately, telling Pedro that it would be a privilege. Pedro and the Senhora were delighted. The boys were to be taught mathematics, history, astronomy, geography, the Roman alphabet, and analytical thinking. They would start by learning to read and write in Portuguese.

Pedro was pleased to think that the boys would have an education, but he was still deeply troubled. He loved them dearly, and had always had a good relationship with them. He dreaded that relationship being damaged or destroyed when they learnt the truth about the slave trade and that he, who had instilled Christian principles into them from an early age, was actually involved in it. Both boys were becoming more inquisitive about what was happening at the fort – especially Carlos. He was asking questions, some of which Pedro found difficult to answer. Soon, they would learn about the slave trade from Ibrahim. How could he justify his involvement to them? The boys were fair-minded. Would they understand? No, probably not …

Ibrahim suggested, that instead of teaching them to read and write, he should begin by teaching them about slavery. He thought that it would make it easier for Pedro if they could understand that slavery was integral to life in Africa. First, he would teach them about 'Slavery in the Domestic Economy' then he would introduce them to the 'Transatlantic Slave Trade'. He would

take two neighbouring kingdoms as examples: The first would be Benin, the kingdom least involved in the transatlantic slave trade, and, the second would be Dahomey, one of the two kingdoms most involved in it. Pedro was still anxious but he hoped that the boys would, finally, be able to accept the world from which they had been so carefully shielded.

When the boys went for their first lesson, Ibrahim was sitting in the shade in the men's courtyard. They greeted him politely and sat down at his feet.

'Before we start', Ibrahim said, 'I need to find out how much you know. For instance, do you understand the word "economy"?'

After a muttered consultation, the boys replied that "economy" was about money and about buying and selling things.

'Yes, that is right' said Ibrahim 'The economy is a kingdom's supply of money, a large part of which comes from trading in foodstuffs, livestock and merchandise. However many of the kings have an even bigger source of income. Do you know what that is?' The boys looked blank. 'Most of their money these days, comes from selling people. Slaves' He looked down at their startled faces.

'How can a king sell people who don't belong to him, Sir?' asked Tom.

'They do belong to him Tom, because they are his slaves.'

'Well, what exactly is a slave, Sir?' asked Carlos.

'Although he is a person, a slave is also a commodity. He belongs to his master, and he has to obey him.'

'Like your parents, Sir?' Ibrahim smiled.

'No Carlos, It is nothing like your parents. The slave owner does not love the slave. He only wants him for work or for profit. Parents love their children and care for them until they are grown up. Slaves are slaves until they die, until they escape or until they are freed – that is called manumission – and it doesn't happen very often.'

'But, Sir' asked Tom 'how can you buy a man? I don't understand. Could I buy Carlos? How much would he cost?'

They both giggled, but Ibrahim did not look amused.

'Concentrate please. Slavery exists throughout Africa. There are a huge number of tribes in West Africa who are constantly fighting each other. The winning tribes take everything from the tribes that lose. They chain their captives up and, if they don't want them for themselves, they sell them as slaves to another kingdom, or, if they are not too far from the coast, to the 'Merica ships.' The boys were looking anxious and Carlos suddenly interrupted, sounding upset.

'Now I understand. That is what happens here, isn't it Sir ?' he said. 'I knew that something bad was going on here. The ships take people from down there.' He pointed towards the barracoons and turned to Tom. 'You know Tom – that is why we are sent out on Adventure Days. I am sure of it. My mother doesn't want us to see what is happening. When do they come back to Africa, Sir?' He was close to tears. Ibrahim was taken aback at the intensity of his reaction. He realised that, to be so het up, Carlos must have been agonizing over slavery for a long time.

'Try to keep calm, Carlos. Very few have ever come back to Africa.'

'That is wrong, Sir. What about their families?' asked Tom.

'I am afraid that is the way it is' said Ibrahim. Then, changing the subject. 'Look at this, I have drawn you a map of the Americas. That is North America and that is South America,' he pointed. 'They are divided between four nations: France, England, Spain and Portugal. Portugal owns Brazil, a big country in South America. Many of the Ashanti slaves are sent there, others go to North America.' He pointed again 'The West African kings are becoming immensely wealthy from the sale of slaves, and the white nations are becoming immensely wealthy from their labour.'

Carlos groaned again, 'Portugal and Spain … my grandfather was half-Spanish. I am called after him.'

'Yes, Carlos, but, you must keep calm. This is not your family's fault, nor is it about just two countries. After Spain and Portugal, the Dutch became the biggest traders, then the British and the French, who still take almost half the exported slaves for the Caribbean islands. They have slave posts on the Ashanti coast, so do Denmark, Sweden and Prussia.'

Ibrahim was worried by the boys' naivety. All their lives, they had lived in a slave fort, surrounded by slaves, with slaves being shipped across the Atlantic from only a few hundred yards further down the coast. They were right-thinking, intelligent, unsophisticated, and young for their age. The more Ibrahim talked about the slave trade, the more upset they became. He could not help wondering if the decision to shield them for so long, had been a wise one, particularly for Carlos, who, had become convinced that, he was, in some way, to blame for the slaves' suffering. Tom loved and respected Pedro and the Senhora but had never thought of them as parents. His mamma-woman had told him everything she could remember about his parents. His father had been a king and she had been a maid to his birth-mother. As he grew up, he was never sure which of his memories were real, and which she had instilled into him. He was, by nature, self-controlled, but Ibrahim could see that, he, too, was deeply affected. Both the boys needed time to adjust.

'Now, Carlos, your mother has a beautiful statue. She will have told you where it came from. Do you remember where that was?'

'Kingdom of Benin' chorused the boys.

'Quite right. Now, I will tell you about Benin. Personally, I think that the Oba of Benin is, probably, the most enlightened of all the West African kings.

'The Oba of Benin, Akenzua I, is regarded as both a king and a god. He has absolute power. He has made it illegal for men from his kingdom to be sold to the 'Merica ships. He sells slaves and prisoners to European countries but not to the 'Merica ships. The Oba is the only king who appears to understand that to sell a generation of the kingdom's youth is to sell the kingdom's future – and, likewise, to sell a generation of West Africa's youth is to sell West Africa's future.' Ibrahim frowned.

'A moat and a high defensive wall surround the City of Benin. It is ten miles long,' said Ibrahim. 'Inside the wall the houses are of a regular design and each one of them, is said to have its own private well. It is a good place to live. The city is well-governed so there is almost no crime. The people live in luxury and peace which is why they have the time to make the statues. The aesthetic appeal of their statues is second only to the famous Ile-Ife bronzes from the Oyo Empire. They do not have the same naturalistic perfection but, nonetheless, they are fine statues.'

'Do they have some like my mother's?' asked Carlos

'Yes,' said Ibrahim, 'Statues like your mother's, only bigger, surround the Oba's palace and plaques depicting soldiers decorate the walls. They all symbolise power.'

Ibrahim knew that the boys would find Dahomey's part in the slave trade much more distressing. He was worried about Carlos who had begun to look uncharacteristically depressed. He decided to speak to Pedro and ask him what should be done. When he heard Pedro coming down the steps on his evening rounds, he came out of his room.

'Good evening Sir, May I have a word with you, please?

'Good Evening Ibrahim, has anything gone wrong?'

'Please come in Sir, I need to talk to you.'

Pedro went into his room and shut the door 'What is it Ibrahim?'

'Both the boys are finding the concept of slavery difficult to accept, Sir. It might be better if they had a few days off.' Pedro, knowing that Ibrahim must have been exceptionally worried to have suggested such an idea, asked 'Both of them or Carlos?'

'Mostly Carlos, Tom hides his feelings.'

'I thought so. Thank you, Ibrahim, We will stop their lessons for the time being and I will talk to the Senhora and come to see you again tomorrow evening.'

Pedro and the Senhora, at once decided to send the boys out for two days of physical activity to calm them down. Ibrahim would finish teaching them about slavery, as soon as he could, to allow them to focus on less unpleasant subjects.

The following day, as well as their usual guards and minders, Pedro sent two other servants to accompany the boys. One was a proficient climber who was to teach them how to climb coconut palms, and the other was the fort fisherman who would teach them to fish with a harpoon. By the time they had mastered the technique of climbing to the top of coconut palms, they were looking happy and relaxed as they dropped coconuts down to be taken back to the fort. There was no time left that day to go fishing, but they felt refreshed and were looking forward to fishing the next day. When they arrived back at the fort it was time to go to the Senhora's courtyard. They had no time to think or talk about slavery until they were in bed. By then they were so tired that they fell asleep almost immediately.

Two days later, it was time for their final lesson about the slave trade. 'Dahomey' Ibrahim told them 'is a very rich kingdom and, like Benin, it is well run. The King has a women's army, trained to protect him and to keep order. The previous King, King Agaja, conquered two new kingdoms, the Kingdom of Allada, and the Kingdom of Ouidah (Whydah) The two conquered king-doms provided him with thousands more slaves and a very valuable Atlantic port – Ouidah. From there they export at least a thousand slaves every month' Poor Carlos had begun to look guilty whenever slavery was mentioned.

'It is wrong. Why can't they stop it?' asked Tom.

'No-one can stop it. It is morally wrong, of course it is. By any standards, the African kings who sell the slaves and the English, Portuguese and the other European nations who buy them are committing crimes against humanity.

'Is Carlos right, then, about the ships in the bay?' Tom asked.

'Yes, I have no doubt of it. A few slaves go to Europe but, from here, they are usually taken on the supplies ships. We will look into that too. But not today.'

◄◄ 10 ►►

Slavery had become the boys' obsession. They shared a room, and talked late into the night. Except when they were out on an Adventure Day, they thought about nothing else. The more they learnt, the more they wanted to know. They had decided to find out everything they could, in the hope, one day, when they were grown up, they would be able to bring the slave trade to an end.

After the lesson on Dahomey, Ibrahim started teaching other subjects. It was a relief, both to him and to the boys. They were learning arithmetic and to read and write. In history, Ibrahim was teaching 'The History of Africa – North of the Equator before the Transatlantic Slave Trade'. The boys particularly enjoyed these lessons. Ibrahim had begun with the country in which they lived – the Ashanti Empire. They were fascinated by the size of the army, the soldiers, their weapons and their armour. They were particularly interested in the Sika Dwa Kofi, the sacred golden stool of the Ashantis. Ibrahim told them that the word 'Ashanti' meant 'because of war' and that before going into battle, the Ashanti generals would always consult the sacred stool. Every lesson ended in a clamour of questions. 'Was the Sika Dwa Kofi made by the Supreme Being? How did the generals know what the stool was saying if it could not talk? Why did the Ashanti Empire need such a big army?' and many more questions. Lessons on other African countries ended in the same way. Questions, and more questions. 'Why Was Mansa Musa so rich? Were the Egyptians giants or why were their temples so big? Why were the Christian churches in Lalibela built down not up? Where did the horsemen of Bornu get their armour? Could Ibrahim take them to see the Sika Dwa Kofi? Could they have a chariot? And a horse?'

The answer to all their requests was

'No, sadly, no' Ibrahim had drawn a picture of a chariot being pulled by a horse. 'You need roads for chariots.'

'We could make them. it would be easy.' Said Tom

'No. A long time ago the kingdoms did breed horses, but not to pull chariots. The kingdoms do not allow strangers to cross their land without permission. If they had roads, it would be easy for people to go wherever they wanted and that would destroy their security.

'Why would it, Sir?'

'Because, think, if there were roads, hostile tribes would make use of them to plunder other kingdoms. The horses were used for raids on neighbouring kingdoms, or to exchange for slaves. One horse would buy ten or twelve strong men and even more girl slaves. Now, as I have tried to explain to you, every able-bodied human being is at risk. Especially, young and strong men like you two.'

Ibrahim knew that it was all too common for young men, seeking unsupervised freedom, to be kidnapped by gangs, and dragged off to the nearest slave post, but the boys were reluctant or, perhaps, too nervous to accept the dangers.

'How could they,' Ibrahim asked himself, 'have lived all their lives with minders and armed guards constantly in attendance and, yet, still be so ignorant?' On reflection, he realised that it was precisely because the boys had never known anything else. To them, being sent out with minders and armed guards was just part of their normal lives.

'You are well looked after but you must be sensible. As I said, it is dangerous everywhere along the coast.' He spoke emphatically.

Although, they thought the slave trade abhorrent, Ibrahim had made them want to be part of the outside world, whatever the risks. They were teenagers and the more they learnt, the more trapped they felt.

◂◂ 11 ▸▸

Eventually, as they grew up, the excitement of their adventure days began to wane. They had learnt to swim under water and to dive amongst the beautifully-coloured fish on the reef. They had raced each other up palm trees to fetch down coconuts and dates. They had learnt to shoot with bows and arrows, to throw a spear, to fish, to track wild animals, to rock climb and to hide themselves either in trees or in the undergrowth so that they could not be found. At nearly sixteen, they were experiencing the confusing thoughts and feelings of adolescence. The joy of being away from the restrictions of the fort was tempered by the fact that they were being supervised. They were fond of their minders, but they wanted to go somewhere – anywhere – where they could be together without constant supervision. They wanted action. They wanted to broaden their horizons. They wanted to meet people, people of their own age both boys and girls – Yes girls. What were girls? They hardly knew. The youngest woman in the fort was Tom's mamma-woman.

They complained to each other, and to Ibrahim, that they were bored. Ibrahim was unsympathetic. He had created a small library of texts for them on the expensive paper imported from Portugal.

'You have all those texts that I have written for you. Instead of complaining about being bored, you should study them and concentrate on learning as much as you can. You will not always have the opportunity to learn. The more you learn, the better it will be for your future lives.'

Despite everything, they knew that they were lucky, and that however disgruntled they felt, they still had each other, the family, the community and Ibrahim, all of whom loved them. Even when they felt grumpy, they never quarrelled with each other.

Pedro and the Senhora were worried. Pedro had suggested sending the boys to his brother in Portugal, but the Senhora would not hear of it. She trusted no-one else to look after them. She was convinced that they would be taken as slaves if they left the safety of the fort. They were tall and strong and with their looks, they would be a valuable catch for the slavers. Along the Ashanti coast there were, already, nearly sixty slave posts, each one of which posed a risk to those travelling either by land or by sea. If they were sent to Portugal on a cargo vessel, the captain might sell them to a slaver, or his ship might be boarded by pirates. It was not safe.

Pedro decided, once more to consult Ibrahim. He had fleetingly wondered, if, even though it was so far away, it might be possible to send the boys to Mali and sign them up at the university. Ibrahim shook his head.

'Although Malians of different cultures live peaceably together in Timbuctu, only Islamic students are accepted at the university. Some Timbuctu people are Dogons. Their religion is ancestor worship. We, the Malinke people have a mixture of Islamic and African culture. It would be impossible for the boys because there is no Christian community there. Also, you must understand that, although they are in danger from the transatlantic slave trade here, Timbuctu is the hub of the Arab slave trade. From there, the slaves are taken to Morocco, Algeria, Lybia or Egypt. Others go to Europe or The Levant. I suspect that more than half as many slaves again cross the Sahara to North Africa as cross the Atlantic to the Americas. Neither of the boys, particularly Tom, would be safe there, especially as there is no suitable community to look after them.'

'Yes I understand' said Pedro.

'I think, then, that I shall take them back to Portugal. Even there, I worry about Tom's safety. I think that I can protect the ladies, the Senhora, Miriam and Tom's mamma-woman easily enough, and Carlos could just about pass for being Portuguese, but, Tom couldn't. A good-looking young African like him could be at risk. By the way, Ibrahim, if we do leave, and if I could arrange for you to go back to Mali would you have somewhere to live?'

'Oh yes Sir, I could live with my nephew in Bamako, but it is a long way Sir. At my age, I do not think that I could travel that far without several stop-overs.' Pedro remembered the soldiers.

'Would you like me to petition Kusi Oboadum, the Assantehene. You remember that when you first came here, he sent the Palace Guard to collect you? I could tell him that you have educated our boys and that you are now well enough to travel? He has sons who would benefit from your teaching, and I understand that the Palace staff at Kumasi are very well treated.' Ibrahim looked thoughtful.

'Yes that might be a good idea. The palace is very luxurious. We had a most enjoyable time when we stayed there before I was abducted. They seemed to be decent people.'

'If that fails,' said Pedro, 'you can stay with us. There is an anti-church movement in Portugal which means that the Jesuits are losing their power. It will make life slightly easier for Muslims. Providing you lived with us, I think that you would be all right.'

'You have saved my life, Sir, and I thank God that I was abandoned here. I am very grateful to you and to the Senhora but I think that if the Assantehene needs a tutor for his children, that would be more suitable for me. Also since Ashanti captured the kingdoms of Dagomba and Gonja there has been a big Islamic community in Kumasi. I would easily be able to live with them if the Assantehene did not want me.'

Pedro felt a sudden rush of affection for the old man.

'Thank you, Ibrahim. I feel that we owe you a great deal more than you owe us. Our boys' lives have been transformed by your teaching. Their prospects are now much better than they were.' He bowed and turned quickly away.'

Pedro intercepted one of the army coastal patrols to ask them to convey his petition, (a manuscript, beautifully written by Ibrahim) to the Assantehene. Within a month he had had an answer. The Assantehene had been delighted. He had eagerly agreed, and had replied that he would send Palace Guards to collect 'the Honoured One' at the end of the year. He would have his own quarters in the palace and he would teach the Assantehene's sons. Pedro had always suspected that Ibrahim had not told him everything. 'The Honoured One?' Ibrahim? What did that mean? He handed the message to Ibrahim who read it and bowed.

'Thank you Sir' he said 'That is satisfactory.'

Pedro was none the wiser.

It was to take Pedro much longer to arrange for his family's return to Portugal. In the meantime, he was still looking for ways in which to improve the boys' lives.

He gave them a fishing boat and, for a short time, accompanied by the fort fisherman, they enjoyed providing the fort with quantities of fish but, even out at sea, they were followed by armed guards in a second boat. His next idea was to allow them to mix with the merchants who trekked up and down the Ashanti coast, earning their living from the slave posts. Several times a month, some of them would come and lay out their merchandise behind the fort. They were, at least, a link to the outside world, for which the boys were yearning, and the guards would be there for their protection. The boys were excited. Some of the traders wore turbans, which, they thought rather scary. But their fears soon faded at the prospect of being able to talk to people from different places. In a mixture of broken English, Spanish, Portuguese, Arabic and Akan, the traders regaled them with tales of their misadventures: of the wild animals, of the poisonous snakes, of the water holes drying up in the hot weather, of the camels' bad temper, and of the brigands attempting to ambush them or to steal their camels.

Two of the traders brought gems, wood carvings, leather bags, decorated belts, knives, spears, and cutlasses, all of which fascinated the boys. They also brought sweets – chunks of a soft toffee filled with chopped up almonds. Carlos loved these. He had a sweet tooth and he wanted to know how they were made.

'Sugar,' the man said.

'Sugar? What's that?'

The man stared at him in astonishment. Carlos watched as one emotion after another crossed the man's face. What was wrong with him? Carlos

had only asked him to explain a word. The man finally calmed down. He said:

'I bring you some next time.'

With that, Carlos had to be content.

That day, after talking to the traders, the boys went up to the battlements to watch them leave. The traders strapped bags on to their saddles, and set off on their camels. Six slaves walked behind them. They were in chains and had iron collars round their necks. Behind them walked an ugly-looking man with a whip. The boys had not seen them when they were outside. They were shocked. They looked at each other

'What's going on?'

'Who are those poor men?'

'Where are they taking them?'

'Why is that man hitting them?'

The slaves did not look like bad people, in fact, they had looked not unlike people from Tom's tribe. They were tall, as he was, and could easily have passed for his older brothers. What had they done wrong? Why did they have to wear chains? Why did that cruel-looking man whip them? The boys' world changed in that moment. They were beginning to understand what Ibrahim had been trying to teach them.

They went to find the Senhora.

'Mamma, why did those slaves wear chains?' asked Carlos.

The Senhora had dreaded this moment. She knew where it would lead 'They are not slaves from here. They are from the Dutch fort. The traders have been paid to guide them to the Sanwi Kingdom. There has been some sort of quarrel. I am not sure exactly what happened.'

'But why the iron collars round their necks? And the man with the whip …?' Carlos persisted.

'Sit, we have to talk' said his mother. 'Listen to me and try to understand. We live in a bad and dangerous world. I came here in chains. My father was killed and our tribe was enslaved. I came here a slave. Your father rescued me. He had to pay for me. If he hadn't bought me, Carlos, I would be a slave in America and you wouldn't exist.' Carlos looked cross. She turned to Tom. 'We try to make a happy life here for everyone, but, all the staff, even you and your mamma-woman, came here as slaves.'

'Did you have …?' Tom put his hand to his throat.

'Yes, Tom, and so did your mamma-woman, only her neck collar was taken off so that she could carry you.'

The boys looked at each other in dismay, disgust etched on their faces.

As Ibrahim has told you, all kingdoms use slave labour. That is how it is. My father had them, at least sixty of them, perhaps even more. Most of the time they were happy. They lived together with their families.'

Carlos asked. 'Did my father put those collars on their necks?'

'No, as I said, they came from the Dutch fort at Elmina.'

'What about those people who are put on the ships?'

'The people are slaves and, yes, they are brought here in chains, and they leave on the ships.'

'Well we must stop it. We can't let that happen. It's so wrong.' Carlos sounded distraught.

'Why doesn't my father stop it?'

'He can't Carlos, it is his job. This fort is a slave fort.'

Carlos jumped up. 'Christianity says "Do as you would be done by." Father is always telling us that. No-one should be chained up like that. It is wrong. They looked so miserable. I will tell him …'

'Don't …, Carlos. Nothing can be done. All we can do is to try to make our lives and our servants' lives bearable.'

'Were the servants slaves too?' Carlos asked.

'Yes, of course, I have just told you, except for you and your father, we all were. Your father paid for Tom and his mamma-woman too.'

Carlos was looking more and more distressed. He kept repeating.

'But it is so bad, so bad, we have to stop it now …'

His mother spoke again, 'Wait, Carlos. Listen to me. For the slaves that stay in Africa like the ones you saw, it is bad, but it is not as bad as the 'Merica ships. The 'Merica ships are the worst, that is why we do not allow you out by yourselves without a guard.'

'Yes, Ibrahim told us. What work do they do in 'Merica?' Carlos asked.

'They are forced to work. Cotton, Sugar, baccy. They are beaten and badly treated. Carlos remembered the strange reaction of the trader when he asked the meaning of 'sugar'. That was it. The slaver knew that slaves, possibly from the fort's own barracoons, were making sugar which then came back to Africa to make those delicious sweets.

'But, how do you know?' Carlos asked his mother.

'People talk – the traders all know what goes on, and the two boys from Dahomey.'

'What boys?'

'Two young fishermen. They were on their way home with their catch, when they were kidnapped by a gang of slavers. They were sold as deck hands to a 'Merica ship. After two years, the ship came back to Africa. They were chained up, but there was a storm and the ship hit a rock and sank. They escaped. Nobody knows how, but two days later they came ashore. They told everyone how they were treated in America. The boys were not lying. Great ridges ran down their backs where they had been whipped.'

Carlos hid his face in his hands and moaned. 'But … my father … he is part of this. How could he?' His mother shook her head. 'No, no, no, Carlos, He is a good man. 'Your father does not own this fort. He cannot say what is to happen. It is owned by the Portuguese government. Your father works for the government. He didn't ask to come here. He was sent here.' Carlos looked perplexed then said, 'But why? He didn't have to.'

'People who work for the government are not given a choice, Carlos.'

'That's enough for now,' said Senhora. 'Try not to think about it. Say your prayers. We will talk again – perhaps tomorrow.' She looked tired and sad.

◂◂ 12 ▸▸

The boys ran to their room and lay on their beds. Carlos curled up like a wounded animal. His words came out in a groan.

'My father … How could he? How could he do that to those men? Those chains …' Seeing his distress, Tom sat beside him until he heard Pedro shut the chapel door. Then he left Carlos and went to the Senhora's courtyard. He knocked at the gate.

'Come.'

He went in, closing the gate behind him. He did not speak. The Senhora sat looking at her bronze statue. She looked up, 'Hello Tom, is everything all right?' He shook his head. 'Carlos?'

He nodded.

She stood up and came over to him. 'Go to your mamma-woman. I will stay with Carlos tonight.'

She touched his face. Tom bowed and went down to find his mamma-woman. Everything in his world had changed, but, at last, he knew the truth. That night, he watched with a fresh pair of eyes as the servants danced. They were slaves. They had lost everything, but they looked happy. They were singing and dancing and looking as if they had not a care in the world. He admired them.

Back in their room, Tom spoke to his mamma-woman.

'My father – did he sell people to slavers?'

His mamma-woman, taken off guard, stayed silent.

'Please, Mamma, I must know. Did my father sell people?'

'Your Babba – good man, looked after slaves. Only bad men go to 'Merica ships. Your mamma kind lady. Now you not king.' She had been a teenager, probably about ten years older than him, when she had become his mamma-woman. Despite her lack of maturity, she had done everything she could to protect him He touched her cheek. 'You are the best mamma-woman.'

◂◂ 13 ▸▸

Carlos had been shocked beyond anything that his mother could have foreseen. He was mortified to think that his father, the man that he loved so much, should be part of this terrible trade. His mind was in turmoil, and worse still, he feared that it might have alienated Tom, who was known by everyone for his kindness and goodness. Carlos hardly dared to look at him, he felt so ashamed. Tom could feel Carlos's conflict between his love of his father and his hatred of cruelty. As far as Tom was concerned, Carlos was his brother. He loved him and he wanted to help him.

'Carlos,' Tom touched his arm.

'I talked to my mamma-woman. She was my birth mamma's slave. She said that my father's kingdom had slaves. She told me that my father sold them. Some to other kingdoms and some even to the 'Merica ships.'

He frowned and shook his head as if he too was struggling to cope with being the son of a slaver.

Carlos was relieved. He grabbed Tom by the arm and pulled him into their room. It was a hot day. They sat on the cool stone floor while they struggled to come to terms with this new reality. They felt that they should have found it out for themselves years before, but the Senhora had been too clever. She had made quite sure that they had been shielded throughout their childhood.

Carlos had talked to his mother late into the night and she had told him everything that she knew.

'As Ibrahim said, it was my father's country who started it,' he groaned.

Tom said, 'Yes, man, but it wasn't Pedro. It wasn't your father. You mustn't blame him.'

'Who is to blame, then?' asked Carlos angrily.

'Calm down, man, we have to think.'

The boys looked at each other. It didn't make sense. How could good men be involved in such cruelty?

'What else did she say?'

'She said that they are worried about us and our future. My father is going to retire. She said that, probably, within a year, we will leave the fort and go to Portugal.'

Tom looked surprised. 'Really? Will you?'

'Yes. You, too, Tom and, of course, your mamma-woman. They want you to stay with us for ever, and I wouldn't leave here without you anyway. They know that.'

'Thanks, man, nor would I ever leave without you.' For a moment their expressions softened. 'So tell me, what else did she say? Why weren't we told the truth?'

'Because my parents wanted us to have a happy childhood. It is as simple as that.' He looked at Tom. 'Actually, we did, didn't we?'

Tom nodded and smiled. 'What else? Who brings the slaves to this fort?'

'Black slavers paid by the Portuguese Government. The Assantehene, Kusi Oboadum, also uses this fort. Sometimes, he sends some of his soldiers on raids with the slavers. Occasionally, the Whites go too, but they die so easily from the fever that they usually prefer to wait on the ships.' He paused. 'The Whites have muskets. That's how the Ashanti army gets them. The Assantehene swaps them for slaves – especially with the Dutch.' Carlos was calming down. 'If we try to understand everything about the Slave Trade, we might be able to make it stop. Ibrahim will probably be able to help us. Let's go and find him.'

Ibrahim was sitting in the sun in the men's courtyard. He looked up as the boys came in. He was expecting them. 'So, your questions have been answered and it hasn't made you happy?'

'How can we stop this trade, Sir? We need your help,' Carlos said.

Ibrahim looked up to see anguish in the boys' eyes.

'Try to understand, dear boys. This is way out of our control. If the slaves were not brought to this fort, they would go to one of the other slaving posts along the coast. If this fort closed down, it would make no difference to the slave trade. The men who run the forts are responsible only for providing a staging post for the slaves before they are shipped. Your father, Carlos, has to obey instructions. We must pray that the trade will end, but there is absolutely nothing we can do to stop it. There is hope for the future, because important people in several of the white countries are doing their best to have it abolished.'

Tom spoke, 'What I don't understand is why they take our people, not other countries' people, 'why are we are so easy for them to buy? Why can't they take from their own countries?'

'As you already know, slavery is part of West Africa's domestic economy. That means that most of the kingdoms have slaves that they can sell. The white countries do not have slave economies. They did, in Britain, until the Norman Conquest. After that they had serfs, who were not owned, but their lives were no easier than those of slaves.'

Ibrahim continued.

'Allowing the best of our young people to be sold as slaves decreases, not only our prospects, but the status of black people in the eyes of the white nations. If, instead of fighting each other, the kingdoms between the coast and the Sahara were to unite under a central government, we could create a wonderful society. We would prosper as one nation, protected from foreign invaders by a national army. As things stand, the kings make fortunes for themselves by selling slaves. The only thing that will stop them is if the whites stop buying. We must pray for that.'

◂◂ **14** ▸▸

Learning about the slave trade had changed the boys' lives. The more they learnt, the more they wanted to know. They had decided to find out everything they could, in the hope, that their knowledge would enable them, one day when they were grown up, to put an end to slavery.

'Sir,' Tom asked 'how did the white nations persuade the kings to sell them slaves?'

'It was not very difficult,' Ibrahim replied.

'The white countries give the kings expensive gifts. It is a form of bribery although they call it friendship. On the coronation of King Haffon of Ouidah, England sent him two whole ship-loads of expensive gifts, including a beautiful Louis XV gold-leafed throne. Portugal gave him, amongst other things, a magnificent crown. Not only do the white countries shower the kings with gifts but they pay a fortune for their slaves. In addition to which, the kingdoms are able to use the 'Merica ships as a prison service. Prisoners are taken to the coast and sold either to a slave post, or directly to a ship. That is a great convenience for the kings when they want to rid themselves of undesirable characters. However bad it is for the prisoners, in some cases, they might be better off on a ship than if they remained as prisoners in the kingdom.' Before the words were out of his mouth, Ibrahim had regretted them. Tom, had his hand up.

'Why would it be better, Sir?' he asked.

In every country in the world criminals were sentenced to death for serious crimes. Ibrahim had been thinking, not of judicial penalties, but of the widespread West African practice of human sacrifice. It was a topic that he had no intention of discussing with his unworldly and sensitive Christian pupils.

Ibrahim looked up. The drums were being brought out into the court-yard. Without answering, he stood up and said: 'Look … there are the drums. It is getting late. You are both good boys. You have good brains and good hearts. If you want to do good in your lifetimes, you must keep your nerve. You will not succeed if you cannot keep calm. Brains not fists. Don't forget that.'

He walked towards the steps. The boys wished him good night and went up to the Senhora's courtyard. What would happen to Ibrahim if they left?

'He will be all right' said the Senhora. 'Your father has already talked to him. He will probably go to the palace at Kumasi to teach the Assantehene's children. Soldiers will come to guard him. Slaves will come to carry him on a litter. He is happy about that.'

'And what about the other servants?' asked Tom. The Senhora looked sad.

'I shall miss them, Miriam and your mamma-woman will come with us and the others will go on working here. The next manager is lucky. We will make sure that he understands that.'

'But we can take our minders, can't we?' asked Carlos.

'No, I am afraid not. They will be all right. The man who is coming to take over is not married but the barracoons are being increased in size. Several of our guards will go down there and your minders will become guards here.'

'Well I am not going then. I am certainly not leaving here without them.' Carlos, shocked and defiant, stamped his foot.

His mother touched his cheek.

'Sooner or later Carlos, you will go out into the world. Is it not better for your minders to have a settled future when you do so? This is an opportun-ity for them. Their tribe was enslaved and their homes were destroyed. Their kingdom no longer exists. It would leave them without a secure position if you boys go away.'

Carlos put his head in his hands. His shoulders were heaving. Tom caught the Senhora's eye and bowed. He left quietly, found his mamma-woman and, together, they went through to the men's courtyard.

SLAVE

A few months later, the boys stood on the battlements watching a ship, anchored in the bay. All the cargo had been unloaded, and the lighter was heading to the mooring when they heard a strange whining noise followed by a splash. Looking down, they saw the heads and backs of two horses. They swam to the shore, trotted up the beach and shook themselves. The beautiful animals had been bought by the Assantehene. Six men were waiting to take them to the palace at Kumasi. The closest the boys had ever come, before, to seeing horses was a pair of mules owned by one of the traders. They had been quite different from these beautiful prancing animals.

'Come on' said Tom. 'Let's go and have a look.'

They ran down but they were too late. The horses had been led away. They had been taken to a disused barracoon which Pedro considered safe from animal and human predators. Armed guards would ensure their safety until daybreak. Pedro saw the boys' disappointment.

'Quick, run to the garden tower and you will see them going by.' The boys ran but all they saw were the backs of the horses and their grooms disappearing down the track.

The following day was a loading day and, predictably, an Adventure day. The boys were looking forward to going out. They knew that their minders would stop them from going to the barracoon to see the horses, so for the first time ever, they plotted to play truant. They were now determined to think for themselves and to make their own decisions. They considered that they had been over-protected for far too long.

'Let's wait until they're not looking and then run for it. We'll only stay for a few minutes to see the horses and talk to the men.'

'Yes. No-one will know except our minders.'

'They won't tell. They would be much too scared.'

'I know, but we don't want to get them into trouble.'

'We won't stay long. We might never see horses again.'

No-one, other than their minders, would ever know – that's what they thought.

Early the next morning, as they left the fort, the minders walked ahead, talking to the guards. Tom and Carlos looked at each other. Perfect. Just what they needed. Gleefully, they fell back, then, barefoot and silent they turned and ran towards the barracoons. The minders, still talking, believed them still to be following. They could, already, see the horses, outside waiting to be saddled, when, as if from nowhere, came men – white men – lots of them. The shocked boys were wrestled to the ground. They hardly had time to call out before they were knocked unconscious, dumped in a boat and ferried out to the waiting ship. They felt nothing. Their minders arrived at the shore to see them being man-handled on to the deck. They splashed into the sea and started to swim. The anchor was weighed, the sails hoisted and the ship glided quietly out into the Atlantic. Futile though it was, the poor young minders went on swimming. They swam and they swam, and they swam.

◄◄ 16 ►►

The boys regained consciousness to find themselves shackled in the hold. Their heads were throbbing and, at first, neither of them could understand what had happened. They were shackled to each other. Next to each of them lay a stranger, also shackled. There was a terrible stench which made them retch. They were sweating. It was boiling hot. The creaking and groaning of the vessel made their headaches worse and they were thirsty, desperately, desperately thirsty. When they realised what had happened, the shock and grief were so great that for the first week they could not speak, nor even look at each other's swollen and reddened eyes. What idiots they had been. The realisation that it was entirely their own fault overwhelmed them with guilt and misery. What had they done? Not only to themselves, but what had they done

to Tom's mamma-woman? To Pedro, to the Senhora? To Ibrahim? To Miriam? What had become of their minders? Hell had engulfed them. The pain and misery were almost unendurable. Every time they closed their eyes, they were haunted by their grief and by searing guilt for the grief they had caused to the people they loved.

They were on a French ship, the *Henri IV*. Both the captain and most of the crew were French. Daily, the slaves were allowed on deck for five hours, to eat yams or rice and beans and to take exercise. Now that Tom and Carlos could look at each other again and could talk, they, gradually, became accustomed to the misery and degradation. They were sickened by the behaviour of the crew and of the captain, but their spirits returned, and feelings of shock and humiliation changed to feelings of fury and contempt. Who were these less-than-human people who could treat others in such a shameful way? The sailors hit the slaves with knotted ropes to make them jump around, to keep fit enough to fetch a good price in the American slave market. Infuriating though this was, it gave the boys an idea. The ship was still sailing along the coast to collect its final cargo of slaves, before turning away from Africa to sail the Atlantic.

Tom and Carlos remembered the drums in the men's courtyard. They decided to try drumming together with their heels, to see if the slaves would respond. That afternoon they tried it out, and one or two of the slaves looked at them questioningly. Every day they repeated the drumming and, day by day, more and more slaves began to show interest. They had recognised that the rhythm was asking a question. Word passed from slave to slave and once they had understood, they responded without hesitation. What was the question the boys were asking? The question was 'Shall we mutiny?' What was the answer? The answer was an enthusiastic 'Yes.' None of the crew suspected these strange dance movements. Tom and Carlos, although younger than many of the slaves, were physically taller and stronger. They were soon recognised as their leaders. Tom, more so than Carlos, because of the colour of his skin; Tom's skin was black like theirs. Carlos, to their eyes, was suspiciously pale in colour.

In the hold, instructions passed along the rows of shackled slaves. Their plan was that, when they were brought up on deck, the slaves would pretend to fight. Slaves fighting each other was so rare that, with any luck, the captain and crew, would be taken off guard. Then, at a given signal the slaves would start shouting – all one hundred and forty-seven of them at once – the resulting noise and confusion would allow Tom and Carlos to grab the captain, take his gun and throw him into the sea. Without him, a shot or two fired over the heads of the crew would, they hoped, ensure their cooperation. That was the plan. Had they not been so frightened, they would have laughed. Enslavement had cut short their boyhood. They were adults now and they were planning to lead a mass escape.

'Brains not fists.' They remembered Ibrahim. Self-control, rigid self-control. Survival was their priority. Survive and escape. Forget the past. Shut away memories. Only allow yourself to think about the mutiny – only the mutiny. Nothing else.

◂◂ 17 ▸▸

That evening the ship sailed towards the coast. It was to collect more supplies and fresh water from the river before loading the three hundred slaves, being held on the beach. As they exercised that day, Tom and Carlos studied the coastline. Of particular interest to them was a towering rock formation which stretched across one end of the bay. It was extensive enough to provide protection for all of them if they reached the shore. Back in the hold, Tom gave the signal. Tomorrow was mutiny day. In response, one by one, the shackles fell silent. The slaves had understood. The boys could feel their excitement, and they even heard the unfamiliar sound of a nervous giggle.

The next day the ship anchored off the coast. The slaves waited tensely for the hatches to open. Nothing happened. They waited and waited. They heard the shouts and curses as slaves were loaded into the next door hold. They heard the anchor chain being hauled up. They felt the movement of the ship as it set sail. Forty minutes later, the hatches opened. Their plan had failed.

Utter misery overwhelmed them. Shackled once again in the hold, the boys knew what they must do to preserve their sanity. Close their minds. Shut down. This corrupt and depraved trade would destroy them if they let it. Tom reminded Carlos of the secret world of their childhood. They whispered to each other, reliving every one of the stories they had invented as small children – once again, losing themselves in the comfort and seclusion of their imaginary world. Soon their stories passed from slave to slave as they lay in disgusting squalor, shackled together in the creaking vessel. The slaves' enjoyment of the stories encouraged Tom and Carlos to invent more. Carlos had a particularly lurid imagination which made his stories popular. Tom and Carlos would survive. They were together.

A few days into the voyage a major storm broke over the ship. A whole day they lay, unfed in the vile-smelling hold, as the ship pitched and plunged in the waves. Finally, the hatches were opened. The sea was calm, and the sun was shining. This time, for fear of losing too much of his valuable cargo, the captain allowed them to stay on deck for longer than usual. They were fed with beans, barrels of herrings and yams, and were not tormented into taking exercise. Four weeks had passed since they had left Africa. Sickness was wide-spread. Many were dying – both amongst the slaves and the crew. Every morning, the dead were stacked in piles before being thrown into the shark-infested ocean. Tom and Carlos were shocked at the lack of respect for the dead, and, aghast to see that it was not only the dead, but also the sick, who were casually thrown into the sea. The boys stood, their heads bowed, as they prayed for the souls of the dead, and for their spirits to return to Africa.

◂◂ **18** ▸▸

For nine weeks they sailed, before the ship put in at Jamaica, only to find that another slave ship had recently left. No more slaves were needed. From the deck the boys watched slaves cutting sugar cane. It was their first sight of working slaves. After another four weeks of rough seas, they reached Charleston in South Carolina. A lighter barge ferried them ashore. Washing, fresh sea-air, food, imprisonment in the barracoons ready for the next day's auction. 'A cargo of 320 Negros for Sale' One hundred and seventeen had died on the crossing. The slaves, half-naked on a platform, were subjected to humiliating scrutiny. Cold unblinking eyes stared, as white hands prodded.

To be bought and owned by another human being? Like an animal? It was happening just as Ibrahim had described. 'Brains not fists'. They could not use their fists anyway. They were manacled.

'Close your mind, man,' Carlos was chained to Tom.

'Hyenas,' Tom muttered. Then came the most devastating moment of his life. Carlos was unchained from his side and pulled away. Carlos struggled so hard that he broke one of the catches on his manacle. It was not enough. He was dragged off. For a second, their shocked eyes met. Then Carlos disappeared from his sight. Tom felt that a knife had been driven into his heart. He could not remember a single day in his life when they had been apart. Yet, somehow, neither of them had foreseen this eventuality. Grief flooded his being. Could he survive without Carlos? In his mind, he saw his face and heard his voice, 'Brains not fists, Tom, brains not fists'. He could survive, and he would survive.

Before sunrise the next day, manacled on a horse-drawn waggon, Tom and three other men were driven to a cotton plantation. They had been bought by a well-dressed man, but his overseer was dirty and smelt of drink. It was the overseer who drove the waggon. When they arrived at the plantation, late in the afternoon, the overseer was in need of another drink. He took them to the slave enclosure. He pointed out the cabins and the whipping post stained with African blood, and then, just for the fun of it, he cracked his whip, flicking Tom's back. Tom did not react. Furious, the man raised his whip again but then let it fall. He needed a drink. 'Just you wait,' he threatened, and, locking the gate of the compound, he released the guard dogs and departed to his quarters to spend the night in an alcoholic haze.

As they heard the overseer's door bang shut, slaves appeared from their cabins. Speaking quietly, they greeted the newcomers with great kindness. They gave them cold cooked yams and water laced with rum. Tom hadn't spoken a word since being parted from Carlos. He still didn't speak, but he saw kind faces and accepted the food and drink put into his hands. He considered starving himself to death, but that would mean breaking his promise to Carlos. He must stay alive and strive for freedom. Not just for himself, but for every African forced into slavery against his will.

Day followed day of back-breaking work. Ten hours of picking cotton. The lash, endlessly flicking from one back to another. Not for any reason – just because the overseer felt like it.

Day after day, week after week. Month after month. The slaves gave Tom companionship and friendship. They knew that he needed time to recover. Once he had learnt to live with his grief, he found himself with new friends, their shared affliction binding them close. He and two others escaped. He led the posse away from his companions enabling them to go free. He was recaptured, punished and sold to another plantation. After a month, he escaped again, and was, again, recaptured and punished. All his childhood he had been loved, cherished and nurtured. The suffering that he had been made to endure changed him for ever. What he would do, or where he would go, he did not yet know, but he could feel a new energy driving him relentlessly forward. Strength, courage and determination flowed through him. He would never submit to this tyranny.

◂◂ **19** ▸▸

After his second escape, Tom was sold to a tobacco plantation near Wilmington where he was befriended by an elderly woman slave. Her name was Nmula. She introduced him to the other slaves, and told him that, on the following day, a Sunday, the slaves would be going to church. Most plantation owners persisted in the, almost invariably vain, hope that, by sending them regularly to church, their slaves would, eventually, become less rebellious.

The next day, the slaves, manacled in pairs, with their feet chained and a central chain linking them together, were walked to the church by the overseer. Tom enjoyed the service. He loved the music and the poetry of hymns, Christianity had always resonated with his thinking. He prayed for the people he loved, for his beloved mamma-woman, for the Senhora, for Pedro, for their minders, for Ibrahim and for all the servants. Through prayer he linked himself to them in spirit. He prayed for Carlos, wept, and prayed again.

Tom became aware that they had an ally in the white pastor. At the end of each service, the pastor was polite and deferential as he bade goodbye to the plantation owners and their families. The moment their conveyances had disappeared, his demeanour changed, and, having collected a box of sugar plums from the vestry, he would sit on the church steps, giving plums and comfort to the slaves and their children, particularly to those whose loved ones had died or been sold. Small children surrounded him. They sat on his lap or leaned against him, comforted by the sound of his gentle voice, and, of course, hoping for more sugar plums. The slaves stayed with the pastor until the overseer returned to attach them to the central chain. The timing depended on his Sunday alcohol consumption. Heavy drinking, Tom thought, seemed to be a characteristic common to overseers – anyway to the three he had encountered.

Tom liked reading but reading matter was banned and education was banned. Tom was surprised when, after one Sunday service, Nmula told him that she wanted to teach him to read English. Tom was perplexed. He had learnt to read in Portuguese. He had not had much chance to read since his enslavement but he did not think that reading English would be a problem.

The following Sunday, while the pastor talked to the slaves on the church steps, inside the church, with the help of a King James Bible, Nmula taught Tom to read not only English but, more importantly, the code used by the slaves' freedom network. To be an agent, he had to read and understand it. News and information came south, brought by network agents. Some were East coast sailors. Others were barge slaves on the Mississippi River. From East and West news travelled throughout the southern states.

As a white 'Man of God' the pastor was trusted and valued by the plantation owners and their families. It was a convenient situation which enabled him to help escaping slaves without fear of discovery. In the church, he had emptied the vestment chest and replaced the vestments with clothing, dry biscuits, pieces of rope, knife blades and anything else that he came across which might be useful to a fugitive. Such was his commitment that he would, confidently, use the network code during his sermons, even in front of the plantation owners. It was through him that Nmula had first heard of the Dunmore Proclamation. The Proclamation offered escaping slaves freedom in return for military service in the British Army. The pastor had begun his sermon with the words: 'My brothers and sisters, open your hearts' (code for 'listen carefully – important message coming through'), 'the King of the World and His Angelic host is here among us' (the British Army is in America). 'They march throughout our land' (they are coming south). 'They are calling on you to fight against evil' (they want you to join the army). 'Make haste to join the angelic host to reap your reward' (Enlist as soon as possible to attain your freedom). 'My brothers and sisters, hear my words' (message over). He continued to the end of his sermon and, then with a beatific smile on his face, he closed his eyes, clasped his hands over his chest, and lifted his face towards heaven.

Nmula was old. Her lined face, and her kindly demeanour disguised a strong and determined personality. She was trusted and valued by the plantation owner and, particularly, by his wife. She was, also, an important member of the slave freedom network. She and the pastor were always the first to know what was happening, where it was happening, and when it was happening. They both knew where slave strikes, escapes, arson and riots were being planned. They knew how many posses were out searching for fugitives, and they knew in which direction they had been sent. They understood the Colonists' political grievances, and were kept informed of the manoeuvres of both the British and the Colonist armies.

Nmula had worked in the house since she was a child and she was loved by the owner's wife and her children. She loved them too. She had nursed the unhappy wife back to health from the point of death and had cared for her and for her children, as the poor woman's mind deteriorated. The poor woman had married a man who, after their marriage, had inherited a plantation. Raised in Delaware, she was a sweet and gentle Christian soul, who hated slavery. She was deeply troubled by her husband's involvement. Constantly depressed and in tears, she depended on Nmula. She told her everything that she had heard, and from whom she had heard it. Had she known that Nmula was an important part of the network, it might have consoled her, but she was too emotionally damaged to keep a secret, so Nmula could not risk confiding in her.

Dave, an African delivery driver, was one of Nmula's most helpful informants. He delivered to the plantation every week. From him, she learned of an escape route being planned through the Appalachian mountains and valley. Dubbed 'the underground passage', it would eventually be a safe route, north, to freedom in Canada, and south to Florida. Dave was heading the team charged with the northern route. It was being constructed through the dense undergrowth which covered the floor of the Appalachian Valley. Another route was planned through the mountains.

Dave told Nmula that he was looking for someone, courageous and altruistic enough, to risk his life establishing refuges and safe houses across the North Carolina plain. Fugitives from the Eastern plantations were faced with two major hurdles before they could reach the safety of the underground passage. The first was the more than two-hundred-mile expanse of plain which stretched from the sea to the mountains, interrupted only by the Piedmont Plateau. The second was to cross the mountains, without being ambushed by the native trackers.

Nmula said 'I got one, he will come.'

She spoke to Tom. 'They need your brains Tom. Why don't you help them first and then enlist. They are risking their lives and so would you be – you know that. If you want to go, they will meet you at the church tomorrow. But I warn you, you must be careful – really careful …' To Tom it was such an interesting idea, that his eyes lit up.

'Yes. I'll go. Of course, I will. I can join up after that,' he said.

Nmula nodded.

'I said you would …'

◄ ◄ *20* ► ►

The next day, while the overseer was distracted by a delivery of his favourite liquor, Tom escaped. Sometimes, the overseer was given a 'present', which he accepted greedily and unquestioningly. He knew that it came from Nmula. She was a favourite with the boss, who had, once, threatened him with dismissal for questioning her. The overseer was convinced that Nmula liked him, and that was why she gave him presents. Not once did he make the connection between her presents and the subsequent discovery that slaves were missing.

Tom was watching from his hiding place. The overseer collected his present and hurried back to his cabin clutching the bottle under his shirt. It was time to go. Once again, Tom offered silent thanks to those who had taught him to climb coconut palms. Unless bound or chained, few walls had the power to confine him. This one had spikes on top, which served to secure the lasso that he held over his shoulder. A few minutes later he had cleared the spikes and was running towards the church.

At the church, Dave locked the door behind him;

'Welcome, man. If it's locked, we will be safe. Even the posses think twice before breaking down God's doors. I am Dave, meet Jordan, he is part of the team.'

Tom thanked him and greeted Jordan. It was a good hiding place. During the day, so many people came and went that their scent invariably lured patrol dogs to the church door, but if the door was locked and the pastor's chiltepin pepper, thoughtfully, ground into the floor of the porch, the dogs were easy to call off. The men were safe.

While the men sat in the windowless vestry waiting, Dave described the planned escape routes. The one going south to Florida, had existed for a long time. Previously, it had led to the Spanish settlement for freed slaves at Fort Mose near St Augustine. The settlement had come to an end when Spain swapped the land, on which it was built, for the island of Cuba. The Spanish had left Fort Mose taking with them a few hundred former slaves. Before the British took over, the remaining slaves had fled to the swampy area of North East Florida. There they joined the Gullah, a community of escaped slaves and their descendants who had joined forces with the Seminoles. The community welcomed fugitives.

‹‹ 21 ››

Dave explained that a recent settlement of Quakers had built their homes on the plain between the Great Dismal swamp and the Piedmont Plateau. They were mostly small-holders who worked and lived as a community. They had developed a ruse to help fugitives. Pretending to be slave owners, a group would travel north, escorting escaped slaves from Quaker settlement to Quaker settlement, until they had crossed into the northern states. Dave had earmarked six of the Quaker houses on the plain and he wanted Tom to ask the owners if they would allow their homes be used as safe houses. Tom agreed enthusiastically. Other than a couple of hiding places provided by Quakers on the Piedmont Plateau, the only protection from the posses were the summer storms or the River Fear, which had saved many a strong swimmer. In fine weather, it was easy enough for posses to recapture slaves on the plain. Hundreds of fugitives including Tom had been re-captured there.

An hour later, the posse and the dogs were at the church door. Ten minutes after that, they left. The men waited another hour, then locked the church door, and having put the key back in its hiding place, walked through the night without stopping. They were in sight of the first Quaker house when they heard the bloodhounds unexpectedly close. They ran as fast as they could, and to their surprise, as Tom put his hand out to knock, the door opened and they fell inside. Although it was so early, the owners, an elderly man and his wife, were already up. Without speaking, they went out slamming the door behind them. The men were bemused. Were they to be betrayed? There was a noise outside. It sounded as if the garden had been invaded by hogs, and so, it had. The elderly couple were chasing their hogs, bloodhounds were baying, and men were shouting. The posse watched in amazement as the old couple apparently tried to round up their herd. The pungent smell of terrified hogs confused the dogs, and the patrol, bamboozled by this eccentric performance, called them off. Ten minutes later, the old people opened the gate to let the hogs into their pen. Then they came into the house, and with much merriment, introduced themselves 'Ma and Pa Prentice, that's us, or just 'Ma' and 'Pa' will do,' said the old lady as she bustled around getting them a drink.

Dave and Jordan left having arranged to meet Tom six weeks later.

Ma and Pa Prentice were delighted when Tom suggested that their house should be used as a safe house. Although they were old, they were fit and strong and like all Quakers deplored slavery. Tom and Pa Prentice spent the afternoon constructing a fugitive hiding place out of a long, narrow store room. They stood a wardrobe in front of its door and removed a panel to make an entrance through the back. When it was finished, Ma Prentice tried it out for herself, going in and out, while she made up her mind what was needed for the comfort of the fugitives.

Pa insisted on driving Tom to the next Quaker house in his waggon. It was a long way for the horse to go there and back in one day but it was owned by one of his cousins. To Tom's surprise, the new couple agreed without hesitation to be a 'safe house'. It might, he thought, all too easily, put them in danger. They were older than Ma and Pa and Tom was concerned for them. Not all fugitives were good people and the posses could be aggressive. Pa, having wished Tom goodbye, returned home. Tom stayed to help the old people construct their hideout. In all his time on the plain, Tom only once found himself in serious danger. He had left the fourth house when he heard dogs and, to his dismay, the distant thud of horses' hooves. No-one could out-run a horse.

'Please God, not again …' Terror-fuelled adrenaline sent him racing to the river. At the edge, he dived in, and swam underwater to the other side. He hid in a bed of rushes, in the nick of time. Looking back, he saw two white men on horseback, one of them carrying a gun, two Africans and five dogs. They were searching the river bank. As their prey (Tom) was nowhere to be found and the dogs were being threatened by alligators, they called them off and went on their way. Tom pulled himself out of the water, and lay panting in the sun. It was a while before he could muster sufficient energy to swim back across the river. Two weeks and many miles later, Tom had visited all six houses. All six were now safe houses. Tom was touched and impressed by the courage of the Quakers. They were taking huge risks. After visiting the last house, he took advantage of a week of bad weather to reach the mountains where he met Dave. He heard that in the last month, far more fugitives than usual had reached the mountains from the plain. Unfortunately some had been recaptured by native tracker teams as they crossed the mountains into the valley. The trackers would lie out of sight, waiting silently, for hours at a time, to catch their next victim. More work needed to be done. Tom started on it the next day.

◄ ◄ 22 ► ►

The main purpose of the Dunmore Proclamation had been to force the Colonists into surrender by removing their work-forces. Extra troops for the British army had been the welcomed consequence. The response to the Proclamation had been dramatic. Hundreds of slaves had been escaping in the hope of enlisting. The Earl of Dunmore, had had to take refuge from the outraged Virginian slave owners on a frigate in the bay. Plantation owners desperately tried to recapture their missing slaves, but with little success. Tom and his co-workers had already set one hundred and thirty-one slaves on their path to freedom, when, in his enthusiasm, Tom allowed his guard to drop. He started to take risks. Creating false trails over the pass was an important part of his work. He was working on a false trail much later in the morning than he should have been, when one of the trackers crept up behind him and dropped a noose over his head. He was bound and, triumphantly, returned to the posse. Recaptured, he was manacled, dragged back and whipped until he passed out. Then, because it was the third time that he had escaped, his face was branded. The overseer, still not content, had a shackle fitted on Tom's ankle. It had a spike which cut into his other leg unless he moved with great care. He would never be able to escape wearing such an impediment. The overseer had a bunch of keys. Another bunch hung in the big house.

Dragged back to his old cabin, it was not long before Nmula came with dressings and medications. They had been given to her by the poor suffering woman who had heard about his punishment. That night she cared for Tom as he slipped in and out of consciousness. She knelt beside him and prayed for him. He woke up to hear the musical cadences of her prayers, and despite his pain, he felt his spirits rally.

The plantation owner turned a blind eye to Nmula's activities. Although she had a room in the house as well as her own cabin, she could go wherever she wanted, and do whatever she wanted because his wife loved her. He knew that she was irreplaceable. His happiness depended on his wife's happiness and his wife's happiness depended on Nmula. He comforted himself that she was too old and too loyal to be a threat – or, anyway, that is what he hoped.

After four days, Nmula had found the key to the shackle. When she came in, Tom looked at her enquiringly, but she shook her head and didn't answer. His heart lifted. He was already better, and he would escape as soon as he could. He went ten days later. He and Nmula wished each other a sorrowful goodbye, intuitively, they knew that it would be for the last time. Commitment to their mutual cause assuaged their sorrow.

The previous Sunday had been the first time since his punishment, that Tom had been well enough to go to church. Consolation had swept over him as, once again, he had contemplated the cross. 'Pater Noster Qui Es Caelis Sanctificatur Nomen Tuum ...' The words from his childhood came unbidden to his mind. Slaves identified themselves with the man on the cross in a unique and profound way. All of them had either endured or witnessed ruthlessly-inflicted cruelty. They felt that their suffering was His suffering and His suffering was their suffering. He had been killed, but they were kept alive. He had risen from the dead to succour them.

His faith in God gave Tom the strength and the determination to escape for the fourth time.

> 'Four times in the night, I fled from the sight
> Of slave-chain and whip and burning.
> Three times I was caught and painfully taught
> To master again my yearning.
> But my own man and free, I was bound to be
> For all the time I was learning!'
>
> ('King Peters of Sierra Leone' FW Butt-Thompson)

The doggerel kept going through his head as he walked.

Heading towards the Appalachian Mountains, it was cold. Tom moved silently through the woods. He needed to reach the Prentice house before the posses were out. A few hours after midnight he heard a noise. It was unusually late for the slavers. Wild animal? Pumas? Bears? He stood listening. Human voices, he was sure of it. If they were escaping slaves, what were they doing hanging around? The posses would be out at dawn when the scent was still strong. Anyone in this area would be caught. It sounded as if the voices were coming from the path ahead. He moved on quietly, and rounded the corner to see two shadowy figures, sitting on the side of the path. He could see the whites of two sets of eyes. He could tell that they were small as were lots of Africans. 'You gone missing?' he asked. The whites of the eyes moved up and down as they nodded. Tom didn't hesitate. 'Follow me. We must be quick.' He pushed past them, walking fast.

Two hours later they were near the Prentices' house. The sky had lightened when Tom heard a moan. He looked round. His eyes widened. The two men following him were not men at all. They were boys. Not only boys, but twins – identical twins, probably not more than ten or twelve years old. He had never seen twins before. He blinked and looked again. They stood crying as they leaned against each other. It was a pitiful sight and Tom knew, in that instant, that, yet again, his life had been changed by circumstances beyond his control. He carried a stick of sugar cane in his belt. He cut off two sections, and, peeling back the outer layer, he gave the boys one each. 'Here you are. Chew this. You will feel better.' It had never occurred to him that they might be children. How had they managed to escape by themselves? Did they have parents? What was he to do? The first and most important thing was to get them to the safety of the Prentice house. They were sitting on the ground, chewing the cane. 'Come on,' he said. 'We have to go.' He pulled them up, then squatting down, persuaded one of them to climb on his back. Holding the other by the wrist, he set off. Every ten minutes he swapped them over. He had been on his way to New York to enlist in the British Army. But … how could he abandon two children with no one to look after them? A five-hundred-mile hike to New York was, obviously, beyond them. He would have to talk to Ma and Pa Prentice and then think again.

◂◂ 23 ▸▸

It was late and the sun was up when they reached the house. He could hear a posse closing in on them. A spade stood upright in the front garden and a folded quilt was airing on the window sill. Both signs told Tom that it was safe to go in. As they went through the gate, Pa came out of the house. He looked astounded when he saw Tom and the twins. He opened the door and, without speaking, nodded to Tom to go in, and closed the door behind them. He spread hog manure over the path where they had walked and, having swept it aside, he resumed his digging.

Inside the house, the old lady stood up.

'Well, Good morning, Tom.' Then, 'Oh dear, oh dear, what has happened to you and who are these?'

'Good morning Ma Ma'am.' Tom bowed. There was no time to talk. Ma opened the wardrobe door. One by one, Tom picked up the terrified-looking twins and bundled them through the wardrobe and into the dark hiding place. 'Quick, we must be quick. Lie down and keep very quiet.' He replaced the back panel and bolted it in place. Ma shut the door, took the quilt from the window sill, and went into the kitchen. The twins wrapped themselves in a rug and, wimpering quietly, shut their eyes. They had just fallen asleep, when Tom heard Pa greeting the slavers. He stayed still until he heard the old lady's cheerful rendering of 'Set My People Free'. Then he crawled out, leaving the twins to sleep.

'They are sick, Ma, what am I going to do?'

'You stay here, Tom, that's what you do. And what have they been doing to you, those wicked men?' She had seen the still-livid brand on his face.

'It's all right, Ma. I am all right.' They went into the kitchen while they talked.

Ma made custard and a banana loaf for the boys' tea. Tom called them, but they were too scared to leave the cupboard. He had to go back through the wardrobe to persuade them. They kept saying, 'White lady, white lady.'

'Yes,' said Tom, 'This white lady is kind, very kind.' The twins still would not move. He said it twice more before they finally came out and stood behind him.

Eventually, the combination of his cajoling, the smell of banana bread and Ma's cheerful face persuaded them. She signalled to Tom to leave and, putting a large slice of the warm bread covered in custard on each plate, she chatted. 'I expect you like eggs. Pa's chickens lay us three or four every morning. The

Meeting House has bananas growing next to it.' The twins did not speak, but they ate and they ate and they ate, until every crumb of the banana loaf and every drop of custard had disappeared.

Still chatting, Ma Prentice made another mixture and put it in the oven.

'You remember that storm? Well, I was waiting for Pa in the waggon when there was such a loud bang that the poor horse ran away,' (giggle from a twin), 'it gave me such a shock ...' (another giggle).

Ma Prentice had broken the ice. The twins were feeling braver and, soon, with tears in their eyes, they were telling her their story. Their father was dead, and their mother had been sold to another plantation. A 'white lady' had arrived in a buggy and taken her away in chains, leaving the poor boys heart-broken. The boss-man had wanted them as house servants, but there had been a fire. Most of the slaves had escaped. The twins had followed, hoping to find their mother. Miraculously, they had survived on berries, and had avoided capture for three whole days. By the time that Tom had found them, they were so hungry that they were looking for their way back to their plantation.

When Tom came in, Ma Prentice looked at him.

'They've lost their mother; she was taken by a white lady. They need your help.'

Tom stared at her then turned to look at the twins. Two beseeching young faces gazed back at him. 'How about this?' he said, 'You and me. We stay together and we'll see what happens. What do you say?'

The twins grinned and nodded their heads.

Ma Prentice chuckled. 'I guess you got two sons, Tom.'

The next day, Ma and Pa Prentice went to the Friends Meeting House. They were away for three hours during which time Tom and the boys stayed in the cupboard. It was not impossible that a posse might try to break in if they knew that the owner was away. The posse did come, but they had mis-timed their visit and they arrived just as Pa Prentice's waggon came rattling back up the drive. The old people were relieved to find everything as they had left it. Ma Prentice had brought clothes for the twins – two tunics and two pairs of breeches, odd sizes and shapes but the twins were thrilled. They were the first warm clothes they had ever owned. Ma spent the evening taking in the breeches to make them fit, and then boiling the tunics to shrink them. The Meeting Houses had become a distribution place for discarded clothes. Tom was anxious about the twins, but at least, with their new clothes, they would be warmer at night once they had left Ma's care. He wanted to get going, but, in the end, they stayed until Ma had decided that the twins were strong enough to leave. 'Their born hearts are poorly, I seen it before, Tom. You have to wait. They need to rest and to eat.'

◂ ◂ 24 ▸ ▸

Pa Prentice had heard, through the Quaker network, that a battalion of British troops under the command of General Clinton was on its way to capture Charleston. 'In that case,' Pa said to Tom, 'you might be able to enlist in Charleston. General Clinton has created a unit of escaped slaves known as The Black Pioneers and Guides. It might suit you. Worth a try.'

Charleston? Where he had first arrived? Tom shuddered at the memory, but if they could avoid capture and if he could enlist there, that is where they would go. It was much closer than New York. He was sure that, if he carried one twin at a time, they would manage to walk as far as that. If the army turned him down, he would work on the escape route as a guide. It would not be perfect, either for him or for the twins, but Ma had said that she would look after the twins, if they were ill.

He asked Pa what he thought might happen.

'If I did join the army, would they allow the twins to come as camp followers?' Pa did not think that it would be a problem. 'Sure they would,' he said. 'Camp followers come in all shapes and sizes.'

There were many questions, and for the moment, he had no answers. First and foremost he was committed to the twins' care. For everything else, he must hope for the best.

A few days later, Pa Prentice saddled the horse and set off across country to another Meeting House. He was one of a dozen volunteers responsible for spreading news and information throughout the Quaker community. From early in the morning until late at night, volunteer Quakers would be at the

Meeting Houses to assist those in need. The plantation owners and posses made frequent checks, but the Meeting Houses had their own spies, and the volunteers were usually busy with innocent pastimes when the patrols arrived.

That evening, Pa Prentice returned home, to tell Tom that General Clinton had withdrawn from Charleston and was on his way back to New York, but that he had arranged for the Royal Navy to patrol the coastal waters. They were to look out for and pick up fugitives from the swamps, then take them North to join the British Army near New York.

After some thought, Tom made up his mind. He said to Pa:

'I think I shall go Sir. I am sure we could get through the swamp and it would be easier for the boys if they didn't have to walk too far.'

'Tom,' said Pa, 'you must be very careful. You have to know where to tread. The Great Dismal is not far from here but it is not easy to cross. It is very dangerous. I don't think that there are alligators but there are snakes, leeches and poisonous fish – not to mention mosquitoes and a million other insects. In some places the water is deep. The twins could die there. You must get an experienced swamp guide. You must never risk trying to cross the swamps by yourselves.'

Tom nodded 'Yes I understand, Sir, I shan't put the twins at risk.'

'Your team will find a guide for you, and, if you want to contact them, you could use my drum.'

'Your drum, Sir?' Tom was surprised.

Pa pointed to a stool with a frilly cover. Without its cover it was transformed into an African drum made of deer skin stretched over half a barrel. Tom tried it out and was impressed by how good it sounded.

'That's ingenious Sir. May I use it tonight?'

'Of course.' Pa sounded pleased.

They waited till the middle of the night, then Tom went outside and, for the first time since his capture, he drummed a message. Would it work? Who would hear it? It worked. At five o'clock the next morning a shadowy figure approached. The call of a blue jay identified him as a team contact, and minutes later, Tom and the twins, already fortified by Ma's hominy grits porridge mixed with honey, slipped out of the house.

25

The guide led them for several hours, to a ravine, above which towered a rocky plateau, a small section which had broken away from the Piedmont at its formation. It could only be reached through the ravine which was so difficult to negotiate that posses never went there. They preferred to wait on the plain to waylay slaves on their way down. Tom and the twins were to stay there until the next day when the guide could reach them. For the twins, it was tough-going, and it was nearly dark when, eventually, they clambered out of the ravine. Tom lit a fire, and, after eating one of Ma's loaves, the twins fell asleep. Tom woke them early and, by midday, they had reached the top. Laughing with relief, they lay in the sun on the warm rocks, eating another of Ma's loaves and breathing in the fresh air. They could hear neither bloodhounds nor the shouts that usually came from working patrols.

They made their way to the other end of the plateau, close to the descent route. From there, they could see for miles across the plain to the sea. They lay on their fronts and searched every square inch of the landscape with their eyes. One of the twins nudged Tom and pointed. Figures were moving around in a glade, beneath the cliff. They seemed to be building something out of branches. A trap? To catch fugitives? Probably. While they watched, two large black bears came lumbering out of the woods and headed towards the men. A shot rang out. It missed. The bears, although unhurt, were displeased. They attacked. Men and dogs ran in every direction and made off as fast they could. It was a spectacle that delighted the twins who giggled happily for several minutes.

Once the posse had gone, the bears settled down and turned their attention to foraging in the undergrowth. Two hours later, when they had lumbered back to where they had first been seen, Tom decided that it was time to go. Having again carefully scrutinised the plain, they set off down the eroded cliff. Dave's team had attached safety ropes from the rocks at the top down to the tree line. It was so steep that even after reaching the tree line, they had to swing from tree to tree, to prevent themselves from losing their balance or plummeting to the foot of the cliff. Tom stayed between the twins helping, first one and then the other. As they neared the bottom of the cliff, he gave the network call and, to his relief, a man appeared out of the bushes. He was a woodcutter, on his way to deliver logs to a saw mill near the swamp. His waggon had two hidden compartments. The twins were so small and skinny, that he thought that they would both fit into one compartment. As it was nearly dark, it was safe for the twins to ride on the waggon, while Tom and the woodcutter walked beside the horse. The moon was full and bright making it easy to travel through the night. They were to rest themselves and the horse, overnight, at a farm belonging to the woodcutter's uncle. He and his nephew had joined forces to help slaves who wanted to escape through the swamp.

The kind farmer provided them with soup, loaves of bread, hay for the horse, and a comfortable few hours sleep in the hay loft.

When they woke up, the weather had changed. Thunder, lightning and heavy rain made it impossible for them to leave. They had to wait until the worst of the storm had passed. It was still raining when they left, but the weather meant that the posses would not be out. There was no need for caution until they came to the outskirts of a town, not far from the swamp. The driver stopped for Tom and the twins to wriggle themselves into the hidden compartments, and then in this exceedingly uncomfortable manner, they bumped along the road to the outcrop of rocks where they were to meet their guide. The driver pulled the horse up, helped the twins out, and handed Tom a sack, saying, 'Goodbye now and Good Luck, Hide as quickly as you can. You'll need to keep that dry.' Tom thanked him and took the sack. Within a few minutes, they were hidden in the rocks. It was getting dark when the hoot of an owl, apparently from on top of the rocks, made them jump. The swamp guide had arrived.

'You Tom?'

'Yes Sah and you?'

'Cyrus, Greetings all. Let's go.'

Cyrus balanced the sack on his head, and telling them to stay one behind the other, he set off. Tom went last. In the fading light Cyrus moved effortlessly through the swamp. The water was a bit deep for the twins, who stumbled so often that, in the end, it was easier for the men to carry them. Despite their added burdens, more quickly than Tom had expected, they arrived at the island. They were soggy, and uncomfortable, but, otherwise, more or less, undamaged. Cyrus's wife greeted them and a fire was burning. 'Welcome. I am Mary.' His wife spoke in a sing-song voice 'Safe, safe at last, the danger is past' she said, smiling, and introducing them to two other men who were sitting by the fire. They sat down. The twins, damp and exhausted, sat each side of Tom and leant against him. Only the smell of the potatoes roasting in the fire kept them awake.

Cyrus opened the sack and soon, as well as the smell of charred potato, the delicious aroma of roasting maize cobs filled the air. As they sat waiting for them to cook, Mary began to sing 'Oh Happy Day …' The twins, warmed and dried by the fire forgot their tiredness. They jumped to their feet to sing with her. The adults exchanged delighted looks as their voices ascended, beautiful, true and clear. 'You like Gospel?' Mary asked them. The twins nodded 'It is supper time' she said, 'After supper we will sing all the songs that you know. How about that?' The twins smiled happily. The maize cobs and the potatoes were ready. While they ate, the twins talked about the songs they had learnt from their mother. Tom had never seen them so animated. When they had finished eating, they wanted to start singing gospel. The men joined in. When five bass voices boomed out 'Deep River …', Tom had a moment of anxiety, wondering how far such an intensity of volume would carry on the night air. He knew that they were safe as no human being would attempt the swamp at night. When the twins had eventually fallen quiet, Cyrus piled wood on the fire, and they all settled down for the night.

The following day, they had to leave early. They were to be at the sandbank half an hour before high tide, as it was only for two hours during the day, that the sandbanks could be used as a pick-up point.

Cyrus collected a pole. It had a thick length of string through each end to make it easy to carry 'We will need this. You boys go in the middle, I will go in front and your Babba will go behind you, that way you will be safe.' The twins smiled at Tom and he smiled back. It pleased them when he was mistaken for their father. It pleased him too. He had begun to feel like their father. The twins held on in the middle of the pole as they went back into the swamp – it

stopped them from stumbling and when they had crossed the beach, the tide was coming in and the water was already deep. The twins were almost out of their depths but thanks to the pole, their heads stayed above water. When they reached the sandbank, there were three other fugitives already waiting.

A few hundred yards out to sea, a frigate dropped anchor, and a boat was lowered. Cyrus waited with them until the twins were aboard, then, waving cheerfully, he set off back to the island dragging the pole behind him. Tom shouted his thanks and ten minutes later they were on their way to the frigate. Tom and the twins waved to Cyrus's retreating figure. As if he knew, he turned and waved back. He and Mary could have chosen to escape. Instead, they had chosen to stay on the island to free others.

·

SOLDIER

26

It took six days to reach the bay south of Newark. There, it was possible to land without having to confront either the French blockade of New York harbour or the slave owners and overseers who lurked near the docks hoping to recapture slaves – their own or, indeed, anyone else's.

The twins, weakened by seasickness, had trouble walking. It had been a rough voyage and the British lines were still several miles off. They were met by African soldiers dressed in blue coats and black tricorn hats. A motto on their sashes read 'Liberty to Slaves'. They were from a unit of General Clinton's Black Pioneers. They had brought with them a mule-drawn waggon, carrying water and a sack of flat breads. It was enough to keep them all going until they reached the British lines. The sergeant caught sight of the twins, and, as everyone always did, he stared, blinked, and stared again. Then, seeing how unwell they looked, he pointed to the waggon. 'Put them up there.'

When they arrived at the camp, it was late. A corporal guided them to a tent where an English officer took their names. Going through the camp, the boys stumbled along behind Tom. Their eyes were half-closed, until, the fife and drums sounded the end of the day. As if a surge of energy had run through them, their eyes opened, and for a few seconds their heads went up, but, it did not last. They were almost unconscious with fatigue and sickness. The corporal grabbed them one on each arm and half carried them the rest of the way. He deposited them on the ground near the cook tent, and shouted to the camp followers.

'Bags of bones I got here – young 'uns.'

Supper was over, but the camp followers always managed to find food for late-comers. A motherly-looking woman came carrying bowls of gravy and mashed potato.

The camp followers were well-accustomed to caring for exhausted, starving or half-dead Africans, some of whom had walked hundreds of miles to join the army. Some of them even died on arrival, others had to be nursed for several weeks before they regained their health. Seldom, were they as young as these two. 'Don't eat too quickly. I will get you a drink,' said the woman. She came back with hot milk. Tom thanked her. He had to help the twins to eat and drink before they finally slumped into unconsciousness.

'You be needing help,' said the Corporal. 'Thank you,' said Tom. At first, he had felt elated but as it sank into his consciousness that he and the boys were actually out of danger, he felt overcome by emotion and wanted to be alone with his thoughts. The corporal pointed to a tent and, between them, they carried the two boys. The motherly-looking woman put three hessian sacks filled with straw on the ground, covered them with a rough blanket and when the twins had been put down, she threw another blanket over them.

The corporal said, 'Sarge, he say tomorrow stay here, stay with the boys, rest and eat. I will come at dinner time.' Having thanked him again, Tom retired to the tent, grateful to be alone with his thoughts and the sleeping twins.

The next day Tom was up with the call of the bugle. The twins were alive, but they hardly stirred. They did not wake until three o'clock that afternoon. The motherly-looking woman brought a bowl of stale bread soaked in hot milk. Slowly, they began to recover.

◂◂ **27** ▸▸

Saturday morning came and the General arrived to inspect the week's African intake. His aim was to create a unit of Black Pioneers for every British regiment. They were needed as guides, scouts, raiders, stretcher-bearers, supplies coordinators, engineers, trench diggers, and cleaners. It was to this unit that Tom would belong.

They stood in ranks. The General stopped in front of Tom and the twins. 'Your sons?'

'Yes sir. Not born so. No Sir.' The General raised an eyebrow.

'They look young,' he said.

'They escaped Sir.'

The General looked again at Tom. He saw a tall, strong-looking man with a dignified demeanour who had no trouble in meeting his eye. He also saw a recent brand mark on Tom's face. He had to control his feelings of revulsion as he turned away. Seconds later, he came back and, again, stared for almost a full minute at the twins. 'You like drums?' he asked. The twins, unabashed by his scrutiny, nodded happily. The General turned to his adjutant.

'What about using these two for the band? Drummer boys? Eh? They would look good leading the troops, wouldn't they?'

That evening the twins were introduced to the drum major. Soon, they were causing something of a sensation in both camps. In the daytime they were put to work in the kitchens. In the afternoons, they practised with the band. Tom was intrigued to learn, from the boys, that the drums were used to communicate orders and messages, in the same way as African drums. Six weeks later, marching side by side behind the Drum Major, they took part in a full dress rehearsal for the King's Birthday Parade. They came back to the camp, completely exhausted, but brimming over with pride and happiness. Tom was relieved that they had managed so well.

If Ma Prentice was right, they would never recover their health, but for the time being, they were having the time of their lives, and they were popular and over-indulged by the kitchen staff. During that summer, the kitchen staff were hired out to the New York elite to serve at their social events when the regiment was away. On the first occasion that the twins had been part of the team, they had become an instant success. Soon, no New York social event was considered complete without them dressed in their drummers' uniforms, standing on each side of the front door as the guests arrived. Time passed and they grew slightly taller, but never less alike.

Tom soon realized that the African troops regarded General Clinton as their saviour. They trusted him as they had never before trusted a white man. He had created for them a unique environment where they were respected and well-treated. His scrupulous fairness had overcome their fears.

Tom's commanding presence was an advantage in the army. He was a good soldier and a natural leader, strong, reliable, conscientious, disciplined and law-abiding. Thanks to Ibrahim and Nmula, he was far better educated than his compatriots. Liked and trusted by both the officers and the men, he was soon promoted. A year later, he was again promoted. This time he became the unit's sergeant-major.

◂◂ 28 ▸▸

A new camp follower was working in the cook tent. Her name was Sally, and the twins would come back to their tent at night and regale Tom with the jokes she had told them. One night, Tom, who had just finished his rounds, returned to find that the twins were not yet back. He had told them to be in bed by ten o'clock, so he walked over to the kitchens. The twins and Sally sat by the embers of the campfire. Tom watched them for a while then he cleared his throat and the boys jumped up. 'Say goodnight and go to bed,' he said, and when they had disappeared into the darkness, he turned to Sally.

'Thank you, Miss, but you mustn't let them be a nuisance.'

She smiled. 'They are no trouble Sir.' Tom bowed and went back to his tent. His thoughts, which usually centred either on the welfare of the twins, or on those of his troops, had changed direction. What a lovely girl Sally seemed to be. It was now she who occupied his thoughts. A few days later, he decided to do his evening rounds a little earlier so that he could join the twins and Sally for a drink before bed. For several months, thereafter, it became his nightly routine. One night, as they stood up to leave, he said, unthinkingly,

'It's almost as if we are a proper family.' The twins looked at each other and said nothing.

Sally said nothing. Sensing a suddenly highly-charged atmosphere, Tom hastily retired.

Having clamped down on his emotions for so many years, it was difficult to imagine that he could actually have a family life. Sally might not want him anyway. Would it be fair to her if she did? For the next two nights Tom started his rounds later, so that the twins were already in bed by the time he had finished. He thought of Sally and of courtship. What was courtship? He wasn't sure that he would be any good at that. The third night, he went back to the campfire, late, at the twins' bedtime. 'Bed,' he said. His voice was unusually harsh but, instead of following them, he sat down.

'Drink, sir?'

'Yes please, and Sally, please call me 'Tom', not 'Sir'.'

She smiled as she gave him a toddy. He sipped it for a while and then, without preamble, 'Sally, will you marry me?'

Silence.

He looked at her with an agonised expression.

'I'd have to think about that Tom, sir.'

'How long would you need?'

''Bout two minutes, I think,' Sally beamed.

It was arranged. They were to be married. Banns were read in the New York church, rings were bought. They were to be married before the unit left for Newport. The twins were in a state of high excitement. Tom was aware of them plotting and whispering behind his back. He decided not to interfere. He felt so blessed. Sally was far more than he could ever have hoped for and, to his great surprise, she loved him.

The day came. The twins disappeared. Tom assumed that they had gone to help Sally. He set off to the church with the corporal, who was to be his best man. It crossed his mind that the camp seemed rather less noisy than usual. On their way to the church, he saw the regimental bugler. 'What's he doing?' he asked but before the corporal could answer, they heard a drum roll. On either side of the church door stood a twin, drumming enthusiastically. They were both dressed in their ceremonial uniform. Tom caught his breath. What on earth did they think they were doing? Who had authorised that?

'Don't worry, Sah. Cap'n said they could,' said the corporal.

Tom had visualised a quiet wedding with some of the camp followers and the corporal as his best man. The church was full. Only his long experience in rigid self-control steadied him as he walked down the aisle between the smiling African faces. Waiting at the altar rail for Sally, he felt a surge of emotion as a triumphant bugle call proclaimed her arrival. One shock after another. What else would happen on this extraordinary day? He turned round and found out. Sally, looking beautiful in a white dress, was on the arm of the Captain who

was in full ceremonial uniform. The Captain? A beautiful African bride on the arm of a white officer, who, as it happened, was his commanding officer? The twins stood behind them. He could hardly believe his eyes.

Poor Tom. He had, always, so rigorously adhered to protocol. He was stunned. His knees were close to buckling and his emotions close to overwhelming him. He turned for a second towards the cross, then, turning back, watched the procession walk slowly up the aisle. For a moment the two men's eyes met. The captain bowed slightly. Tom bowed back while clenching his fist, to resist his deeply-rooted impulse to salute. The service began. 'Who giveth this woman …?' The captain took Sally's hand and handed it to Tom, then, bowing for the second time, he turned, walked back down the aisle and out of the church.

The service over, arm-in-arm, Tom and Sally were escorted back to the camp by the cheering congregation. The party lasted for half the night. The motherly-looking woman produced a many-tiered iced cake which, cut into very small pieces, was large enough for every soldier in the fifty-strong unit, and for the camp followers. Who had paid? Where had it come from? Sally read his thoughts. 'It is all right, Tom, it's all right. It's for everyone. No money. The Cap'n gave us the icing.' Surprised and touched, he calmed down and looked over to where the twins stood. They grinned when they caught his eye. He laughed. They were, he thought to himself, looking distinctly smug. He wondered what, exactly, they had they been up to?

Five weeks later, his unit of Black Pioneers was preparing to accompany General Clinton to Newport, which was under attack by the Colonist army. Some of the camp followers were to stay in New York to care for the sick and any newcomers. Sally and the twins were among them. The twins would continue to work in the kitchen and Sally was feeling unwell and thought she was having a baby. Tom was relieved that he could leave her and the twins, knowing that they would be safe. The twins were disappointed. The General had talked about drummer boys leading troops into battle. The twins had thought themselves perfect for the job.

It would be a long time before Tom saw any of them again. Months later, when the Pioneers arrived back in New York, he found, to his joy, Sally happily cradling their little daughter, Clairie, now three months old. The little child looked healthy and content. The twins welcomed him noisily. He looked at them carefully and was pleased to see that their health had not really deteriorated too much since he had last seen them.

Tom's unit stayed in New York for only a few weeks before, once again, they were on the move. General Clinton was commanding a campaign to capture the Colonists' headquarters in Philadelphia. However, when the Colonists discovered that the approaching army numbered thirteen thousand, they hastily decamped to York, ninety miles away. Clinton's army stayed in Philadelphia unchallenged, throughout that winter. In the Spring they returned, once again, to protect New York. Tom arrived back at the camp to find his family well. He was able to reassure the twins that, as Philadelphia had been occupied without a single shot being fired so, yet again, drummer boys had not been required to lead the troops into battle.

◄ ◄ **29** ► ►

The war had ended, and, unexpectedly, the British had been defeated. The General had warned his superiors, that their ill-judged campaign would result in defeat. Being proved right did not improve his popularity. A few years before the end of the war, the General had issued the Philipsburg Proclamation. It had promised the ex-slaves, not only their freedom, but, also, land, in return for their military service. The General, himself, had inherited land from his father, and had had every intention of allowing the government to divide it between the Pioneers. It was not to be. At the end of the war, the land was confiscated.

The British were given three months in which to leave New York before George Washington took over. The regiment and the Pioneers were camped side by side waiting for news of their futures – the regiment of their return to England, and the Black Pioneers, of their entitlements. 'Land, Freedom and Equality under British rule' had become a mantra in the camp.

During those months, there was chaos and confusion in and around New York. Thousands of Africans were hiding wherever they could. They all hoped, by some means or another to escape to freedom. Irate slave owners and overseers searched the streets, looking for their missing slaves. Terrified Africans arrived at the camp begging for sanctuary. The General deployed the regiment to surround the unit, and, with his sense of humanity undiminished, allowed the big regimental tents to be used to shelter fugitives. Tom felt an increasing sense of desperation. There was talk of Nova Scotia but, if nothing was organised before the British Army left, many Africans would, undoubtedly, find themselves, once more, enslaved. Tom had been told to visit the officer in charge of the African affairs at least twice a week. He did so, but was constantly disappointed. For weeks there was never any news.

The army was about to leave when, at last, Tom was given the news for which he had been waiting. He was told that the white colonists who had remained loyal to the crown, together with the Black Loyalists, The Pioneers, African soldiers and camp followers, were to become free citizens under British rule in Nova Scotia. 3,000 Africans were on the list and many more wanted to be. Every time Tom left the camp, he was intercepted by Africans begging him for help and asking him to intervene on their behalf. He spent hours listening and trying to help, but he could only advise them. He could make no promises. Promises were not for him to make.

◄◄ *30* ►►

It was the night before they were to embark for Nova Scotia. Tom and Sally were putting out the kitchen equipment and utensils to be shared amongst the departing Africans when he heard the captain's voice.

'Sa'ent major, Where are you?'

'Here, Sir.'

'Come with me, the boss wants to see you.'

The boss? The General? At half past ten at night? Their final parade had taken place earlier in the day and the unit would be disbanded from the moment they set foot on Nova Scotian soil. What could he want?

Tom followed him to find the General sitting at a table holding a pen and staring at a blank sheet of paper. He and the captain saluted. 'Sit down, gentlemen.' The Captain sat. Tom, who had never before sat in the presence of the regimental officers, hesitated.

'Sit Peters, sit. We haven't much time.' He looked over his shoulder and said to a soldier servant, 'Bring port and three glasses. It is cold tonight.'

The servant returned, did as requested and was then dismissed.

The captain poured out the port and, then, looking at Tom, the General spoke.

'You, Peters, have been given charge of the Black Pioneer units in the Nova Scotian counties of Annapolis and New Brunswick. It won't be easy because of the distances involved. I want you to make sure that the Pioneers get the entitlements they have been promised.' He cleared his throat,

'I hope that it will not prove to be too much of a problem.'

He paused, then he said,

'However, it is my opinion that Nova Scotia should only be a temporary solution. I believe that you must have the chance to return to Africa.'

Africa? Tom could hardly believe what he was hearing but the General continued.

'I have been trying to decide how this can best be achieved. I think that your first step should be a petition to the Foreign Secretary in London. It should simply ask for permission to tell him of your experiences. I want you to do that now. I am returning to England and I will take the document with me. There are many Members of Parliament, who would be happy to give you their support. A company has already been formed to resettle Africans in Sierra Leone. The founder is a friend of mine, a Member of Parliament called Granville Sharp. A previous attempt, undertaken for the London blacks, was unsuccessful but, this time, it will succeed. My friend will make sure of it. We believe that it would suit The Pioneers. A Parliamentary Secretary will contact you and I would like you to keep in touch with him.'

Tom felt a mixture of shock and elation. Could this really be happening? Africa? A glimmer of light at the end of a very long tunnel. He stared at the General in astonishment. The General continued,

'The Captain understands the procedure and he writes a fine hand. He will write the document for you. It shouldn't be too long. If it is accepted, we will make further arrangements. If it isn't, you must go on trying until one of them is accepted. Then, when that is approved, you will need to speak to the Members of Parliament in person. I can't bring them to Nova Scotia, but I can arrange for you to come to England.'

They stood up. Tom and the Captain saluted. As he was leaving, the General stopped and looked at Tom.

'I cannot right the wrong that your people have suffered. Please know that I am far from alone in detesting it. I will never let the matter drop. I wish you good fortune.'

Again, Tom felt stunned. After another glass of port and another hour of discussion, the Captain took up his pen. Believing Tom to be illiterate, he was surprised to learn that Tom could write – although not, of course, to the standard of his own immaculate copper-plate script.

Between them, they devised a letter asking that the Cabinet Minister should 'suffer the poor Black to tell his own melancholy Tale.' Tom signed it with a cross, and the Captain, with a flourish, wrote his name underneath it. Tom returned to his tent where he and Sally talked into the early hours.

◄◄ **31** ►►

Over the following months, 3,000 Black Loyalists and many more White Loyalists, arrived in Nova Scotia to start their new lives. Tom and his family arrived late after a particularly tiresome sea voyage. Blown off course, they had ended up in Bermuda where they waited a month for the winds to change. As a consequence, they arrived in Nova Scotia much later than originally anticipated.

Tom had permission for Sally, Clairie, and the twins to remain on the ship until the repairs were done. It would probably take them six weeks The ship was dank and cold at night, but they were, at least, sheltered, which, for the twins, was essential. It meant that Tom was able to give his full attention to his work. The weather was unusually bad for the time of year and he found himself in a country deficient of almost everything that decent human living required. He had charge of three Pioneer units and some hundred other Black Loyalists, many of them ex-soldiers who had joined the British Army late in the war. The pressure on the army towards the end of the war had been so great that escaped slaves had, for the first time, been armed and put in to fight with the regiments.

Tom was responsible for nearly a thousand people in two different counties. The communities were separated at the closest point by a seventy mile stretch of water across the Bay of Fundy. The Annapolis settlement was to be near Digby and the New Brunswick settlement was to be outside St John. Having been warned by the General before they left New York, Tom had asked the Corporal to deputise for him in New Brunswick. By the time Tom arrived, the Corporal had been in New Brunswick for six weeks. Tom reached Digby to hear that a cargo ship was due to cross to the Bay of Fundy, leaving soon after midnight. He made haste to board. He wanted to be sure that the Corporal and the St John's Africans were able to survive before he returned to mark out Brindley Town. To his astonishment, when he arrived at St John late the next day, he found the Corporal waiting on the beach. Tom was delighted and relieved to see him but wondered how on earth he knew that he was coming.

'Heard the drums, did you?' He asked.

The Corporal grinned as they shook hands. 'That's where I live' he said pointing to an old shed surrounded by tents 'I saw the ship. I came to see what was happening. I've got some fish for our supper.'

Together he and Tom spent a week marking out the new town and organising the Africans into twenty teams of ten, half of them to fell trees and cut logs, and the other half to build the houses. Then, having paid a courtesy call on the mayor and local tradesmen, and having promised the Corporal to come back every six weeks, Tom left him in charge and returned to Digby.

On his return, his first task was to try to raise his people's morale. They were African and, although it was Spring, the weather was freezing. The Africans were cold and miserable. Illness, death and depression were bringing them close to despair. Sleet and high winds were damaging tents and frightening their children. Several men had succumbed to pneumonia, leaving their widows and children unprotected. Tom knew that it would be catastrophic if everyone was not properly housed before the winter set in.

The Africans had not had the land that they had been promised, and, to make matters worse, their entitlement to three years' rations had been reduced to only enough for eighty days. Hopes and expectations had been high, obviously too high, and, consequently, their disappointment was all the more difficult to cope with. They were downcast and discouraged. Brindley Town still had to be mapped out, the streets laid and the houses built. Tom visited the trades people in Digby and asked for their help. He was surprised at the kindness they showed. One offered to bring a waggon load of flour and market supplies to Brindley Town twice a week, another offered help, to move logs at the weekends. Reassured, and feeling more optimistic, Tom managed to persuade ten of the Pioneers to work with him to lay out the streets. Luckily soon after they had started, the weather changed. Summer finally arrived making it easier to build and morale improved as the town began to take shape.

Tom had decided, before anything else happened, a large hall should be built. It would be a refuge for those who still had nowhere to live when the cold weather came. When they heard about the hall, the Pioneers' spirits lifted. Twenty of them set to and the hall was built, finished and roofed within two weeks. One of the shop owners in Digby provided them with bricks from a ruined cottage in return for a week of manual labour. Tom had used the bricks to build a fireplace and a chimney. It was safer than the wooden chimneys on the log cabins, and the hearth was large enough for several cooking pots. When it was finished, the widows and children moved in, while their houses were being built. As he had done in New Brunswick, Tom organised the Africans into teams of ten. Each team was able to build a log cabin in four days. Chiefly as a result of his hard work and unflagging energy, Brindley Town and the settlement at St John began to look more like towns and less like building sites or lumber yards before the winter began.

When he had finished his house, Tom collected his family from Port Roseway. Sally, the twins, and Clairie moved into their new home, with another mother and her new baby. Tom stayed in his tent until the other mother's house was ready. He then moved into his first home since the fort. Despite his exhausting, frustrating and difficult work, he and his family had a tranquil and happy home life. He taught the twins to fish and to chop firewood. They caught enough fish to keep the family fed. In the evenings, when

SOLDIER

the fire was burning in the hearth, they sang and played with Clairie, making her necklaces and bracelets out of the shells they had picked up on the beach. Being warm and dry at night improved their health, which had deteriorated in the night-time dankness of the vessel. They were soon looking less sickly.

When all the houses had been built and the hall was no longer occupied, Sally and her friends set up a school. Sally could read and write and she had a good head for numbers. In the evenings, Tom used the hall for assemblies. The Pioneers were delighted. 'The Mess' or 'Clubhouse' as they called it, was somewhere they could be together, and, for a short time, forget the problems of their unrewarding lives. When the winter came, Tom and Sally noticed that many of the men were beginning to look ill. The eighty-day supplies entitlement had ended. The men did not have enough to eat. Most of what they could afford or acquire, they gave to their wives and children.

Sally suggested an evening soup kitchen, if they were able to obtain the ingredients. Yet again, Tom applied to the Digby shopkeepers and tradesmen. He struck deals. Six months of vegetables, particularly potatoes, from the grocer in return for building his new store. Bones and two buckets of off-cuts once a week from the butcher in return for an ice house to be dug in the Spring ready for the Summer. Eight months of bread from the baker in return for the Pioneers building an opulent house for his newly-married daughter, and two fishermen swapped part of their catch in return for a group of African teenagers mending their nets. A rare trust and friendship had developed between the two disparate communities. They worked well together.

The soup kitchen was an immediate success. The twins appointed themselves as cooks. They chopped vegetables, cleaned fish, and stewed meat. Sally, Tom and the twins worked tirelessly all evening. Clairie was allowed to help by washing the dishes. When the food was ready, Tom and the twins doled it out while Sally took Clairie home to bed. Because there were too many to feed at one sitting, they had two sittings a day and each man was limited to four meals a week. It was not long before they began to look more robust. They had more energy and better morale, and, above all, they had a better chance of surviving the winter.

When the authorities heard about the school, they sent along a white inspector. Sally had not thought to ask for permission before opening it. Luckily Tom was there when he arrived. The inspector made it clear to Tom that there were rules and regulations and, that, if the school did not come up to standard, he could close it down. Tom sensed that the man was enjoying his authority and, although irritated by the unnecessary intrusion, he drew himself up and answered every question with haughty, but icy, civility.

The inspector was disconcerted. Never before had he encountered such a well-informed or articulate African. Realising that he had failed to impress, he changed tactics, agreed that the school was up to standard, and brought the interview to an abrupt end. After he left, Sally and her friends could not stop laughing. When, eventually, they managed to speak, Sally said 'Poor man, Tom, I felt really sorry for him You sounded so haughty.'

Tom smiled, 'Stopped him talking down to me, didn't it? At least he didn't find out about the soup kitchen. That might have been awkward.' After years of experience with white people, he had found a means of making the difficult ones hesitate before causing him a problem. He had no wish to offend, but he felt that it saved him time and forestalled the endless complications that followed before a dispute was resolved.

'Anyway,' he said to Sally, 'I learnt it from them. It is the way that some of them speak to me.'

Most of his adult life had been spent trying to right the wrongs his people had suffered. The suffering that he had endured, had hardened him. He had come to expect the same standards of honour and integrity from others as he had himself. It, sometimes, made him a little impatient.

◄◄ 32 ►►

There was no question in the minds of the Africans – The promise of equality under English rule had been broken. They were second-class citizens. The dignity and respect accorded to them when they were in the Black Pioneers under General Clinton were fast-receding memories. Tom had visited the Governor several times, in the hope that he would implement the British land commitment, but, with no success. The Governor had expected to be promoted to the position of Governor-General of British North America. He had been passed over in favour of Sir Guy Carleton, previously Commander-in-Chief of all British forces in North America. Consequently, The Governor had lost interest in his job. He appeared unwell, morose and depressed, He was not in a hurry to fulfil either his own obligations nor those of the British Government.

'It is as if he thinks that Africans just don't matter,' Tom thought to himself. Then, remembering the principles instilled into him by Ibrahim, he expanded his thinking to other communities and had to admit that many of them, also, appeared not to matter. Roman Catholics, Jews and native Canadians had also been excluded from voting, local government and access to the courts. Tom was constantly perplexed and saddened by the government's actions. Despite the talk of equality, discrimination was applied to anyone who was not white, Protestant and land-owning. Roman Catholics had recently been offered the vote, subject to their renunciation of the Pope. The Africans' entitlements had been reduced or ignored. The White Loyalists who now outnumbered the Africans by nearly ten to one, had been allowed to bring slaves to Nova Scotia. The presence of those slaves had been catastrophic to the social status of all the Africans. Tom was dismayed that a British government should allow what, to him, appeared to be dishonourable trickery and deceit. He admitted to himself that much of it could be the result of idleness or incompetence and, unquestionably having the centre of government thousands of miles across the sea was not in anyone's interests.

Tom had written his third petition to the Foreign Secretary to say that 'People of colour,' were, 'injured … by a public and avowed Toleration of Slavery,' and that many of the Africans had 'already been reduced to slavery without being able to gain any redress from the King's court' Neither did they have 'protection by the Laws of the Colony.'

Tom never openly talked of these matters or expressed his opinions, even to Sally, for fear of upsetting her. Sally was pregnant with their second child. Her morale, and the morale throughout the African community were his priorities. Frustrated by broken promises, especially in relation to the land, he decided that the only thing he could do was to go over the head of the Governor, and request a meeting with the Governor-General, who was due to visit

New Brunswick. Tom hoped that this might be his chance to solve the land entitlement problems. As Commander-in-Chief of the British forces, Sir Guy Carleton, although not an abolitionist himself, had refused George Washington's request to return African soldiers to their former slave masters. To him, it was a matter of honour to deliver on the promises made by the British Government. 'Surely,' Tom thought, 'a man of his stature would ensure that the Africans received their entitlements.'

He was courteously welcomed by Carleton who, repeatedly, assured him that the entitlements of the Black Loyalists would be honoured, and that they would receive exactly the same as the White Loyalists. Tom thanked him but left, feeling unconvinced and disheartened. He knew that many of the White Loyalists had already been given farms, and, yet, none of the Africans, in either Brindley Town or St John, had been given so much as an allotment. How could Carleton be so certain? He might issue orders, but who would make sure that they were obeyed? What happened in both Nova Scotia and New Brunswick was the Governor's responsibility. Would he comply? And if he did comply, when would he comply?

A week later, Sally's baby was born. He was a strong and healthy little boy who they named John. Tom was relieved that both he and Sally were doing so well. Clairie and the twins were delighted with the new arrival, and spent every spare minute either caring for him or playing with him. Sally was grateful for their help as John was a wakeful but happy baby.

Time passed, and then more time passed since Tom's meeting with the Governor General. As he had feared, absolutely nothing changed. Finally, after another two years, a land settlement was approved. The hundred-acre plots, originally promised to each family, were reduced to a single acre plot for only a third of the Pioneers in Tom's charge. None of the plots outside Brindley Town were big enough to sustain a family. Dishonourable trickery or sheer incompetence? Perhaps both but, certainly, insulting, after the promises that had been made. The Africans were dependent on either working for the whites – sometimes, as little better than slaves – or on working for the Government, building roads. Their only other alternatives were to hunt or to fish. English charities, with their coffers obligingly filled by plantation- and slave-owning benefactors, became aware of their predicament and did what they could to help the widows and orphans. Nonetheless, discontent and poverty were increasing. The Africans' morale had been undermined by their loss of status, subsistence living, and disagreeable weather. Few of them were happy and most of them regarded the Nova Scotian project as a complete failure.

◄◄ **33** ►►

The St George's Bay Company had been reinvented as the Sierra Leone Company for the re-settlement of Africans. At the General's behest, and with the hope of returning to Africa, Tom had kept in touch with the Parliamentary Secretary to Granville Sharp. The directors of the Company had asked for a referendum to find out if the Nova Scotian Black Loyalists would vote to go to Sierra Leone. Feeling excited and optimistic, Tom travelled from town to town talking and answering questions. Everywhere the local Africans set up networks to collect the signatures of those who wanted to go. Gradually the networks spread, until every African who wished to vote, had done so.

Six weeks later, the results of the referendum were decisive. An overwhelming YES in favour of a return to Africa. The question of who should act as their representative was clear. It was Tom.

With the outcome of the referendum, Tom sent word to Granville Sharp's Parliamentary Secretary and, a few months later, his visit to England was scheduled. The fare had been paid by money raised from the African community. His accommodation while he was in London was to be paid by the Sierra Leone Company.

Granville Sharp's letter had sounded helpful and enthusiastic. The Parliamentary Secretary would arrange Tom's timetable, his accommodation and a guide, to be assigned with him throughout his stay. Tom knew that his family would be looked after while he was away, but he was becoming increasingly worried about the twins' health. They were tiring easily. They were finding the fishing and the wood cutting more difficult and, every day, it was taking them longer.

It would have been discourteous of Tom not to pay his respects to the Governor before leaving for England. It was, anyway, time for his annual visit. He suspected that the Governor would think that the proposed return to Africa was a reflection on him. The colony would lose more than half of its cheap labour through an exodus of those who had been entrusted to his care. Although aware of his lack of diligence, Tom wanted to reassure him that there was no ill-feeling, that it was to be expected that Africans would want to return to their native land, but that some of them actually wished to stay. 'After all,' he thought to himself, 'it was unlikely that the Governor could have changed the Whites' attitude towards the Africans, any more than he could have changed the unpleasant weather.'

Joe, an ex-Pioneer, on his way to the Distribution Centre outside Halifax, gave him a lift from Caledonia. Joe had been employed to drive a waggon between Annapolis Royal, and Halifax. The business had been going well, but after one Nova Scotian winter, the proprietor's wife had become so ill that the man had sold up and paid his debts. He had given Joe the horse and waggon in return for his wages. Joe had been delighted. He, now, had the means of earning a living.

He and Tom sat on the front of the waggon, talking about life in the army. Tom was thankful not to have to walk. It gave him a welcome rest. After reminiscing with Joe, he moved to the back of the waggon, and making himself comfortable on sacks of animal feed, he fell asleep. When he awoke, he began to reflect on the increasing racial disharmony and how it could be put right. Black people had come, half-naked, into the lives of white people. Predictably, the white people had thought them racially inferior. He pictured, to himself, a reversal of roles. What if rich and smartly dressed black men controlled half-naked white men? His mind baulked at the thought. Would they treat them any better? He hoped so, but he, certainly could not be sure. If Africans had equal rights, could they live harmoniously with white people, or was it too late for that? Had too much damage been done? Raised at the fort, with its black, white and brown human components, it was easy enough for him to accept everyone for what they were, but most people grew up in single colour communities. Atavism caused most people to fear those who appeared to be different. Could that be changed? Probably not, but even if their thinking could not be changed, perhaps their behaviour could. Tom sighed at the thought of the problems they faced.

Joe had pulled over into a glade. He unharnessed the horse, and allowed him to graze, while he and Tom sat down to eat. Sally had made them enough food to last at least three days.

'Will you have one like him?' asked Joe, jerking his chin in the direction of Halifax.

'One like him? Oh, you mean the Governor? Yes, we will have one like him.'

'That hasn't been so easy here, Tom. Will it work in Africa?'

'It will work, Joe. It will have to. We need protection. If we don't get it, we might end up back on the 'Merica ships five minutes after we get there. Sierra Leone will be protected by the British – anyway, at first – or we won't survive. It is as simple as that. The British Navy is sending ships to guard our coast line from slavers and the Company is sending a unit of ex-soldiers to protect us from hostile tribes, and, of course, to keep order.'

'I understand,' said Joe, 'that's good.' They finished their lunch, and ten minutes later Joe jumped down and put Neddy back in his harness. Tom went back to his cogitations. Lying, again, on the sacks, his mind wandered back to his years in the Black Pioneers.

Before he had created the Black Pioneers, General Clinton must have known that every slave, offered freedom in return for a military service, would join up unquestioningly. He could, easily, have taken advantage of them, but, instead, he had gone to great lengths to make sure that the African troops were well treated, well fed, well clothed and respected. The General, himself, had selected their white officers, but only after lengthy interviews and brain-washing lecturing. It had worked so well that the African soldiers had considered themselves better treated than the white soldiers, Tom recalled how much that fact had amused them and, also, how it had encouraged them to work as hard as they could to prove their worth and to prove the General right.

He remembered the General's last words to him: 'I am not alone in detesting what has been done to your people …'

The General actually believed that every life mattered, regardless of colour.

◂◂ 35 ▸▸

They had arrived at the turning to the Distribution Centre. Joe pulled Neddy up to allow Tom to climb down. 'Thanks, Joe. I wouldn't want to leave an animal like that. I am pleased for you.'

'Joe smiled and patted the horse. As Tom set off to walk the last few miles, Joe shouted after him, 'Tell you what Tom, Neddy and me will bring you to the ship and make sure Mrs Peters and the children get home safe!'

'That's kind,' said Tom, 'thank you Joe, I shall look forward to it.' He waved and went on his way, wondering whether, in fact, it would be wise to take the four-year-old John on such a long trip. John was a cheerful, happy child but not always cooperative. Tom comforted himself that, with the twins and Clairie in attendance, it would probably work out all right.

After spending the night with his ex-Pioneer friends, early the next day Tom cleaned his boots and made himself as smart as he could before going to Government House. The sentries at the gate might look askance at muddy-booted petitioners. Their uniform boots were, of course, clean and shiny, but seldom came into contact with the muddy roads.

The meeting was as friendly as Tom could have expected under the circumstances. The Governor obviously felt that he should have been consulted by the directors of the Sierra Leone Company before so many decisions had been made. Tom felt partly sorry for him and partly irritated by him.

◂◂ 36 ▸▸

Six weeks later, and again loaded on to Joe's waggon, Tom and his family were nearing Halifax. The road was full of Africans who all seemed to be going in the same direction. Tom was sitting in front next to Joe. 'What is going on here?' he asked.

Joe laughed and answered, 'It's not what is going on here, Tom, it is who is going from here? And that who is you.'

'No …' Tom was amazed. Several hundred people had come to see him off. When they arrived at the quay, Joe stopped the waggon so that Tom could speak to the crowd, He stood at the horse's head to keep him calm.

Tom climbed up on to the waggon.

'Thank you, my friends. With the good Lord's help, this will be our first step back to Africa.'

At the word 'Africa' the crowd erupted into loud cheers.

'Let us pray for God's mercy to carry us safely there.'

The jolly-boat was waiting to collect him. He waved and climbed down to where his family stood. Suddenly overcome, he pulled the twins to him and hugged them. Over their heads, his eyes met Sally's. In the look that passed between them, a question was asked: 'Will they live till I come back?' An answer came with a gentle shake of the head 'No, probably not.' He touched Sally's face, kissed Clairie and John, and then, with a heavy heart, turned and walked towards the rock which doubled as a landing stage. He was about to step into the waiting boat, when he heard Sally's scream, and turning, saw John running full tilt towards him.

'Gum dooo, Gum dooo!' John was shouting.

He was a stout little boy, unsteady on his legs and perilously close to the water. Tom spoke sharply, 'Stop John NOW …' John hesitated, luckily, just long enough for his mother to scoop him up and carry him, shrieking with rage, back to the quay. The twins and Clairie were on the waggon. Clairie jumped down to pacify her brother. He stopped crying when she put him up on the horse and, from there, he waved cheerfully to his father. Tom waved back from the bow of the jolly-boat, and, at that moment, the twins' clear voices rang out. Tom felt goose pimples run down his spine. 'How,' he wondered to himself, not for the first time, 'could such frail young men have such powerful singing voices?'

'Amazing Grace, How sweet the sound …'

It was a new and popular hymn. By the end of the first line, several hundred more voices had joined in. The twins turned towards the crowd to conduct. Verse followed verse. It was difficult to imagine that the volume could increase, but every time they sang the lines, 'My chains are gone. I've been set free. My God, my Saviour has ransomed me …', it rose to a massive crescendo, causing the sea birds to take flight in panic. Through the bones of his head, the horse felt the calming beat of Joe's heart. He had the child on his back and he stood still.

The jolly-boat had reached the ship. Tom climbed the ladder to the deck. He stood at the railings with his hand raised in farewell. He could only just see the twins. They grew smaller the further from shore the ship sailed.

Tom was filled with dread at the thought that he might never see them again. He remembered the impact they had had on the regiment, on the unit, on him and on Sally. He had long since given up trying to change them. They were what they were, good, sweet-natured, cheerful and funny, but a law unto themselves. He had never been able to teach them the importance of military rank. The only man they had ever held in awe had been the Drum Major, their hero, whose mace flourishing had kept them spell-bound for hours. Other than that, rank did not feature in their thinking. Tom winced with embarrassment as he remembered how, after a month or so of married life, Sally had finally told him that the twins had taken it upon themselves to discuss their wedding with the Captain. Even after all these years, Tom felt his face grow hot at the thought. Thank goodness he hadn't known about it before the wedding. The twins had been polite and ingenuous, and the amused Captain had agreed to their request. Sally had been taken aback, but had accepted graciously. Mentally Tom thanked his lucky stars that they had not taken it into their heads to consult the General. He, certainly, would not have put it past them.

◂◂ **37** ▸▸

Tom hated sailing. Every creak and roll of the vessel reminded him of his first Atlantic crossing. He chided himself for being neurotic. The Captain was friendly and he and Tom ate supper together. After a long, rough and, to Tom, tedious crossing, they arrived at Portsmouth in the pouring rain. Tom called in at the harbour master's office. The Harbour Master, who had been contacted about his arrival, sent his son to arrange for a seat in the Westminster coach. The coachman was helpful and dropped him off near the address he had been given, and he found the lodging house without difficulty. It was comfortable, and the landlady agreed for a little extra payment to provide him with an evening meal. She gave him a message from a man called Lucas, who had told her that he had been assigned to Tom as his guide. Lucas? Tom had had a friend called Lucas in the Black Pioneers. He hadn't come to Nova Scotia, although he had been on Tom's list. He wondered if there was a chance … But, 'No, unlikely,' he thought.

The next morning, he opened the front door and as he turned to shut it, there was a bellow from behind him.

'Sa'ent-Major!'

Tom jumped. He could hardly believe his luck. A familiar figure, roaring with laughter, held out his hand.

'Lucas! Hello, man, how are you?' They shook hands. They had a lot to catch up on.

Every day after that, whenever Tom opened the door, Lucas was there, propped against the railings.

'Morning, Tom, Sah, where are we going today?'

Whenever they had a whole day free from meetings, they went to the East End to spend the day with the London Africans at their meeting room. The room had been provided by the Committee for the Relief of the Black Poor. When they had first arrived, Pete, the charity manager, and his wife were stirring a cauldron of soup. They greeted Lucas and Tom effusively. Groups of Africans were sitting at tables either talking or eating. They could have as much soup as they wanted and yesterday's loaves and rolls from three separate bakeries were piled up on the tables. It reminded Tom of the hall in Nova Scotia.

Pete knew about the proposed settlement of Sierra Leone to be led by Tom, and he had also heard of another recently-planned scheme which he wanted to tell them about.

'A young man called Beaver was here last week. He was asking our people if they would be interested in going back to Africa to an island called Bulama. He said that he would be able to take at least two hundred people with him. It probably won't be for a year or so, but he thinks that he can establish a community there living off their own crops.'

'Oh?' said Lucas, 'I hope he knows what he is doing. Will they have any protection?'

'They will take guns and things' said Pete.

'They will need more than that unless the island is deserted. What about the tribes who are living there? What happens to them? Even if the island is deserted, which would be surprising, the tribes will hear about it and one of them might attack from the mainland. It sounds risky, Pete. If they think that they can march in and grab all the land, it will be a disaster. The only way it could succeed is if the British Army checks it out and sets up a safe area with a protective fort. Has he taken advice from the abolitionist MPs? By the way you say he is young, what does that mean?'

'I dunno, about twenty, perhaps a bit more.'

Lucas rolled his eyes. 'Disaster,' he said.

'All right, thanks Lucas,' Pete said, 'I will tell them. By the way, Tom, I hope that it will work out this time for you – that Sierra Leone business.'

'Thank you,' said Tom, 'I hope so, too.'

Pete went on,

'Difficult to understand, doesn't make sense, any of it. Look, I want to show you something.' He opened the storeroom door to reveal several dozen bolts of thick wool fabric in different colours and dozens of knitted scarves.

'See what we've got?'

'You must be feeling rich,' said Lucas.

'No, man. We've been given it by a man from up north. Scotland, I think. You know what? He's a plantation owner. He gives us a lot of money too. Mad world, isn't it? He wants every black person in London to have warm clothes for the winter. He also sent these coats.' He opened another door to show a rail of elegant, second-hand frock coats. 'I think that they belonged to him and his friends.' He looked at Tom. 'Why don't you borrow one for your meetings,

Tom, if we can find one big enough to fit you? Lucas can bring it back when you leave.' Tom looked down at himself. Other than in the army, he had never had the chance to be clothes-conscious, but he could see that his clothes were shabby in comparison with those of the smart Members of Parliament. He was already wearing his best clothes but … he understood …

'Thank you,' he said. 'Have you got a blue one? I would feel good wearing one of those at that meeting.'

Pete brought out three coats. 'These are the biggest, see if they fit.'

Tom tried them on. Only one of them fitted him – a smart dark red one.

'Oh good,' said Lucas, 'me too?' He laughed.

'No,' said Pete. 'You can have yours from the plantation owner's stuff.'

'How do you know that he has a plantation?' asked Lucas.

'He's got an African manservant. Ezra, he told me.'

'But who is going to make the clothes?'

'A tailor, or rather five tailors. He has employed them for as long as it takes, and lots of our people can help with the stitching. They've started already.'

Tom and Lucas stared at each other.

'P'raps he's got a conscience,' said Lucas.

'Maybe,' said Tom.

They went to talk to the Africans who were still sitting at the tables. There were some ex-soldiers, a few were Pioneers, but none, other than Lucas, had been in Tom's unit. A few of them had come to England as slaves. Some, with the help of their British officers, had managed to board vessels with their regiments in New York, others had been taken on as deckhands. The British Navy had been as accommodating as possible in helping Africans escape.

Tom was told about the disastrous attempt by the St George's Bay Company to repatriate the London Africans. Lucas had been one of them. Thinking that he could get back to England if he needed to, he had left his family behind. It had proved a wise decision.

'Why did it fail? What went wrong?' asked Tom. They all had something to say.

'From the beginning, the tribes took our stuff and killed many people.'

'Sickness – so much sickness. Lots of people died from that too.'

'Bad land and nothing would grow.'

'The Whites took the better land.'

'There wasn't enough of anything. Bad organisation.'

'It was so bad,' said Lucas, 'that his ex-servant wrote to Granville Sharp, to say that he wanted to catch the first ship back to Jamaica.' They laughed.

'Could it really have been that bad?' asked Tom, briefly remembering the slaves cutting sugar cane that they had seen from the deck of the *Henri IV*.

'It certainly was for some,' said Lucas, 'it ended when the Temne burnt the town down. They gave us three days to leave. Only seven of us managed to come back to England. Some people went to work on Bunce Island, some went up river and became slavers themselves. Thank goodness I didn't take the children.'

Tom was worried. Some of what he had heard sounded not unlike what had happened in Nova Scotia. He would have to make some more enquiries. As they left, he said, 'You know Lucas, we might be lucky enough to have the chance to go to Africa, but there are still thousands of Africans being shipped to America every year. It makes me feel that bad.'

'Look, man,' said Lucas, 'you need to get Sierra Leone fixed up first. That's your job. The abolitionists, they won't give up. Every month they come to the meeting room to talk to Pete. The young one, Wilberforce and two of his friends. They've been coming here, now, for two years. He will make a difference. He's on the committee, isn't he?' Tom nodded. 'Yes, I met him when I went to that meeting with Granville Sharp.'

◂◂ **38** ▸▸

It was mild and sunny on the day of the committee meeting. Tom, smartly dressed in his borrowed coat, felt a surge of optimism. Lucas had come to his lodgings to collect him and they had time to go through the park where the leaves were beginning to turn. They walked across to see St James's Palace before going to the House of Commons. Tom felt nervous about the coming meeting and was grateful to have Lucas with him to discuss the problems that lay ahead – especially as, having been to Sierra Leone, Lucas had experienced and understood the mistakes made by the St George's Bay Company. He was intelligent and had formed his own opinions about what should have been done. Above all, he was adamant that the Africans had needed more protection – not just against the slavers but also against hostile tribes. He left Tom at the entrance of the House of Commons, with a cheerful wave, saying, 'See you tomorrow, man.'

At the entrance, the Secretary to Granville Sharp was waiting for him. He greeted Tom and showed him into a large and rather dark chamber. It had a heavy-beamed ceiling and oak panelling. There was a long table, at which several men sat talking. At the door, an attendant announced him, 'Mr Thomas Peters.' The men stood up. Tom bowed and they greeted him politely. They were all Members of Parliament except for one, a naval lieutenant called John Clarkson. He was there to advise on Naval resources. Tom had already met Granville Sharp and William Wilberforce in private. Both men had, wholeheartedly, committed their lives to abolishing slavery. Sharp introduced Tom to the other members of the committee, then he and Wilberforce sat either side of him telling him about Sierra Leone. Despite their attentiveness, Tom could not help feeling nervous. So much depended on this meeting. He would have felt happier if the General who, at that time, was not an MP, had been there. To his immense surprise and pleasure, just as a servant had started to hand round a tray of drinks, the door opened and, who should walk in, but the General himself.

'General Sir Henry Clinton' announced the attendant.

Inside the door, the General bowed. 'Gentlemen.'

They all rose to their feet, Tom with such vigour that he knocked over his chair. He saluted. Clinton acknowledged his salute, then came round the table and held out his hand.

''Morning, Peters, how are you? I am so pleased to see you again. Let's hope this business gets done now. Eh? How are those twins?'

Tom shook his head and looked down. 'Not too bad, sir.'

Clinton nodded.

The servant had righted Tom's chair. They sat down – one or two a little surprised at the familiarity with which the General had greeted Tom. Tom felt

his confidence come back. He felt that, although he liked and trusted both Sharp and Wilberforce, if the General was there, nothing that he said would be misconstrued.

The Black Loyalists had been sent to Nova Scotia because of the British defeat. At the time, it was the best that could be done, but the General knew that, to the Africans, it would hardly have qualified as freedom. He was convinced that for them, freedom meant Africa, and nothing less than Africa.

The General's outlook was shared by Granville Sharp. They had been friends for many years. They thought alike and were probably the only two there who really understood the tribulations and suffering of the slaves in captivity, and the difficulties that they encountered when they were freed.

Sandwiches and more drinks were served, and several hours later the meeting ended. An agreement had been reached. The British government would send fifteen ships to transport the Nova Scotian Africans to Sierra Leone. There, they would be protected by the British Navy, but would be free to run their own domestic affairs. The naval lieutenant was to accompany Tom back to Nova Scotia to help with the preparations and take charge of the ships. On arrival in Freetown, he would be appointed as the first Governor of Sierra Leone.

The meeting came to an end and, after saying his farewells, the General said, 'Come with me Peters, I will show you around. You can see how things work here, and then we can stop off at the coffee house.'

After looking round Westminster Abbey and Westminster Hall, they returned to the Houses of Parliament, and went up to the gallery of St Stephen's chapel so that Tom could see its impressive interior and watch the workings of the Commons in session. They stayed only for a short time, then left for a nearby coffee house, where they talked about the war. The General's face lit up when he talked about the Black Pioneers. Every one of the units had been a success.

'I must admit, I was very proud of the Pioneers. You were good soldiers. I think about you all frequently. What do you think are the worst problems for them in Nova Scotia?'

General Sir Henry Clinton

Tom told him about the poverty caused by the Africans not being given their land entitlement and how the colour problem had been exacerbated by White Loyalists being allowed to bring slaves with them to Nova Scotia. Allowing slaves into the country had compromised the social status of all Africans and encouraged the Whites to regard them as a workforce solely for their benefit. Tom confessed that he was, again, expecting trouble from them. The General looked aggrieved.

'I suspected as much. I knew it would not be easy for you, but I didn't think that it would be as bad as that. It's the Britannia complex,' he said. Tom looked puzzled. 'Remember the song?'

'I remember,' said Tom. 'It is good music.'

'Yes,' said the General, 'the fact is that long before that song was written, the slave trade had caused the Whites to feel racially superior. I hope that attitude will diminish in Sierra Leone. I have recommended to Clarkson that he elevate people from your community to positions of authority, equal to that of the Council. It can be done, and it should be done. Clarkson will not be there for ever. He has a fiancée who will be waiting for him back here. When he leaves, I would like to see you employed by the Company and appointed as the next Governor but, …' He shrugged and shook his head. 'Anyway, I hope that you are happy about the arrangements that we made today. Are there any questions you would like me to pursue after you go?'

Tom stared. He could not believe what he had just heard. Momentarily dumbfounded, he was slow to reply.

'Um, Yes, thank you Sir, I am happy. It will be much easier to arrange now that the lieutenant is going to be there. He knows about ships, and with any luck, he will have some influence with the Whites, I am worried about those Africans who will be left in Nova Scotia, Luckily, there are two resolute men who will stay on – friends of mine. They are prepared to take responsibility for some of our more vulnerable folk.'

'Good. Well, keep me posted if you can.'

'I will, sir, and thank you … for everything.' Tom had wanted to express his gratitude in greater depth, but he could not find the right words.

'Remember me to the twins.'

They shook hands. Again, Tom saluted. He was touched by the General's belief in him, but he knew that he would never be made Governor.

On the way back to his lodgings, memories of the Middle Passage haunted him. He desperately wanted the ships for the journey to Sierra Leone to be appropriately and comfortably fitted out. He, again, thought about the Whites. They were bound to resent the Africans' departure. and the shortage of manual labourers. Having another white representative of the British government, other than the not-always-interested Governor, would make his life less complicated.

Back at his lodgings he sat down to think. The committee were all good people and ardent abolitionists but, in the back of Tom's mind, there was a question mark. He couldn't quite identify it, but it worried him. There was a slight feeling that he was being controlled. No, that was ungrateful. Could he trust them? The General trusted them. Africa? A white governor? A colony like Nova Scotia? How much freedom would they actually have? Clarkson had seemed nice and conscientious, but he was young. Would he be a good governor? If not, would it work? The Britannia complex. He started to hum quietly to himself. The music was stirring. He was tempted to shout it out, as loud as he could. 'Britons never, never, never, shall be slaves …' He stopped. Slavery –the memories of it made him feel sick. Protection by the British was the only hope for their survival in Africa. It was as simple as that, and the English Government were paying for it. Well, they should be … 'Quieten down,' he told himself. 'Stop being churlish. It is God's will and it was the French who enslaved you, anyway, not the British. You will never have a better chance.'

◂◂ **39** ▸▸

A week before his departure date, Tom woke with a start. Something was wrong. He could feel it. He fell asleep again and dreamt of the twins. They were talking to him, but he could not hear what they were saying. He woke, once again, with the familiar feeling of dread. He was not there to look after them, and it would take him more than a month to get there. He must leave as soon as possible. He put the red coat into a bag lent to him by his landlady and packed his possessions together with a pink frock for Clairie, thick waistcoats for the twins and a tunic for John – all of which had been knitted by his land-lady's two nieces. He had paid for them and had bought a gold cross and chain for Sally. He took the cross out of its box, touched it, and prayed for his family.

As usual, Lucas was waiting for him. 'Morning Boss!' he yelled across the street and then, 'Hey man, what's the matter?' Tom explained. Lucas was sorry. He had enjoyed his time with Tom. They went together to the coach and Lucas promised to deliver the coat to Pete, return the bag to the landlady and to take Tom's message to the committee members. Tom had not left any unfinished business, but he would have rather taken his leave in person.

He managed to get a seat on the mail coach to Portsmouth. He thanked Lucas and wished him well. Lucas saluted. 'Bye Tom Sah, You will be back one day, I can feel it in my bones, and guess who will be waiting to be your guide.'

Tom smiled. 'Thanks Lucas, I have really enjoyed being with you. And you have helped me a lot. Goodbye now. Take good care of yourself and give my regards to your family.'

For once, his luck was in, and a cargo vessel that should have left for

Halifax the previous day had been delayed by a storm. It was to leave the next day. The harbour master expected the captain to board within the next hour. There were not many passengers, and he was sure that Tom would get a berth.

In the evening, six weeks later, the ship dropped anchor off Halifax. Tom, filled with foreboding, went ashore on the cargo lighter. It was at ten o'clock that night when he reached the ex-Pioneers' house and was told, what he was already knew in his heart. The twins had died. They had been fishing when one of them had had a heart attack. His brother had lain down beside him and held him. Frozen to death, or spiritually unable to survive without his twin, he, too, had died. Sally had woken to find them missing. A search party had found them side by side on the shore. They were brought into the church, wrapped in sheets and buried in the same grave. After the funeral, Sally, Clairie and John were comforted by their friends until Tom could come back to look after them.

After supper, Tom rested a while then, before dawn, he set off to walk. It was a long way. He could keep up a brisk pace for three hours at a time. With occasional lifts, he could probably cover thirty miles or more in a day. As the sun came up, he was picked up by a carter on his way to Caledonia. He arrived home just before ten the following night.

It was already more than six weeks since the twins had died, but the door to his house was opened by an elderly lady. He bowed and thanked her. She lived next door and she left quietly. Tom stood watching until she had shut her door. Sally and John were asleep, but Clairie woke up when he came in. She opened her eyes, saw her father, held out her arms and burst into tears.

Tom stayed at home for a week as they grieved together. Friends visited to remember the twins, the happiness they had given, the sweetness of their personalities, the jokes, the games, the fun they had had as a family. Clairie used charcoal to draw pictures of them on the wall and framed the pictures with the necklaces they had made for her. Tom, remembering one of his last lessons with Ibrahim, took her outside to pick out the twin stars, Pollux and Castor. He told her that from those two stars, the twins would watch over her and John for the rest of their lives. He told her that the stars were special, because, as the twins had been, they were very close to each other.

◂ ◂ 40 ▸ ▸

The following week, Tom resumed the evening assemblies. John Clarkson, the naval lieutenant's arrival was expected at any moment. There was a great deal to do and to discuss. Many of the Africans had changed their minds since Tom had last spoken to them. The majority still wanted to go to Africa, but for some of the more vulnerable, memories of the first crossing had traumatised them beyond reason. Others felt that they were too old or too sick and, as before, those who were already earning a reasonable living, were reluctant to give up for fear of once again being destitute. Some names were added to Tom's list, others were taken off.

Meetings were arranged throughout Nova Scotia. As before, Tom travelled from place to place. Again, he started in St John, and, after two days of talks, he again left the Corporal in charge – this time to interview and list those robust enough to endure the crossing back to Africa. He then spent several days in Birchtown, making speeches and answering questions. Once again people wanted to talk to him about their individual choices. Everywhere he went, he was aware of resistance from the Whites. That included the Governor who, since his return, had refused to see him. Tom had had so much to do that he spent little time worrying about it. Soon the naval lieutenant would arrive and he would be staying at Government House. He hoped that Clarkson would placate the Governor rather than let himself be influenced by his rancour. As he had feared, the White Loyalists were quick to react to the prospect of losing their cheap labour. In an attempt to dissuade the Africans from leaving, they had started a rumour that Tom was plotting to return them to Africa in order to sell them into the slave trade for ten pounds a head.

John Clarkson arrived with the ship on which Tom had originally planned to sail. The voyage had taken longer than expected, and by the time they met Tom already had a rough idea of how many people were hoping to go to Africa. He knew that there would not be enough room for all of them and that some would be rejected on grounds of health.

Clarkson and Tom settled down to make the arrangements together. Tom was impressed by the man's attitude. He was meticulous, conscientious and very efficient. He was insistent that the Africans should be properly cared for on the voyage, that the crews should include cleaners for the sleeping areas, and trained cooks so that the food would be properly prepared. Extra food of a good quality and extra fresh water tanks were to be put on board, in case the voyage took longer than expected. At Tom's request each person was to have a berth and access to fresh air. The ships were redesigned accordingly. Together, Clarkson and Tom interviewed and agreed a list of passengers strong enough to withstand the rigours of, what might be, a very testing experience. Tom hated to see the disappointment caused to those who were rejected. The Members of Parliament had assured him that, if this venture was a success, they would be willing to support a future attempt. He prayed that all those who wished to return to Africa would eventually do so.

There were occasions when Clarkson and Tom did not agree. Clarkson felt that, as Governor elect of Sierra Leone, he should have absolute authority. He was young and inexperienced, other than in naval matters and the responsibility of his appointment weighed heavily upon him. To the Africans, Tom's leadership was not negotiable. As far as they were concerned, he was their king. He knew that it angered Clarkson who was frustrated by their refusal to come to a decision without Tom's consent. Clarkson became angry whenever he felt that his authority was being questioned. Tom wondered if he might have been influenced by the Governor's antagonism. He was concerned at the amount of control that Clarkson wished to exert. At the meeting, Tom had been assured that, in Sierra Leone, they would be free to run their own affairs. Clarkson appeared to think that they lacked the intelligence to do so. Tom worried that their colour and impoverished appearance were being attributed to incompetence and low intelligence. Clarkson's heart was in the right place but his attitude, it seemed to Tom, was that of a benefactor bestowing charity on an inferior race.

Six weeks later, 1,200 Africans climbed aboard the fifteen ships provided by the British government. Excitement grew to fever pitch as they set sail. Two days into the voyage, the weather deteriorated, and for five weeks they endured constant storms and gales. Death followed sickness. Sally was sick and Clairie was doing her best to look after John. Tom's mind went back to the first time he had crossed the Atlantic. Grief, sickness, fear, pain, squalor, death and more grief. His people had suffered and were still suffering. Several people had died on his ship. The other ships, were experiencing similar losses. In the sixth week the skies finally cleared and they sailed towards Africa with the sun shining, a following wind and calm seas. Four weeks later fifteen ships were converging on Sierra Leone. Prayers of thanks and rejoicing rang out on every vessel as land was sighted. Tom's ship and two others arrived late in the evening. He was pleased to see the promised squadron of naval ships, already anchored in the bay. By early the next morning, three other ships, including the Governor's, had arrived. The minute that the Governor's flag was hoisted, a welcoming party rowed out to greet him. Members of the council, with some ceremony, escorted him ashore. Once there, a boat was sent to collect Tom. Sally stayed on board with John. Tom took Clairie with him. He thought that, before the day was over, he would almost certainly need a messenger. As they stepped off the boat and splashed their way on to the beach, more jolly-boats rowed out to the ships to bring the Africans ashore. Tom knew that before very long, several hundred people would be on that beach, all of whom would need shelter and sustenance. Quickly he and Clairie climbed up the hill to look at Freetown.

KING

‹‹ **42** ››

Freetown? Where was it? It did not exist. He and Clarkson had been promised houses, streets and stores, but the only houses to have been built were already occupied by those who were supposed to have built the town. The council administrators, sent by the Sierra Leone Company, were living on their ships with plenty of supplies – some of them were drinking heavily, and they all seemed to be enjoying their leisure. They had already settled themselves into an agreeable life-style, and showed only a modicum of respect for the wishes of the new Governor.

Tom's heart sank. More than eleven hundred Africans would be coming ashore over the next few days. A number of them were already climbing the hill. How on earth were they going to cope? Clarkson was talking to the councillors and Tom could see that he was looking agitated. When he saw Tom, he signalled to him to join them. Tom needed a decision. Without waiting to be introduced, he bowed briefly to the councillors and spoke directly to Clarkson. 'I am so sorry to interrupt Sir, but do you think that those who need help should stay on the ships for the time being?' Clarkson answered immediately. 'Yes, Peters. That is a good idea. You are right. We have a problem. Luckily they have a supply of tents which are not being used. Not enough but we can start with them.' He turned back to the councillors and requested that a message be sent with every jolly-boat instructing the Captains to keep mothers with young children, those over fifty, and anyone who felt unwell, on board. He shook his head despairingly. 'Peters, you had better go down and make sure that they do it.' Tom went, taking Clairie with him. On his way down they passed an endless stream of Africans, singing hymns as they climbed the hill, carrying their meagre possessions.

When he was satisfied that the order had been carried out, he and Clairie climbed back up the hill. He had expected to find his people waiting there, but what he saw was the back of a procession of several hundred Africans, singing cheerfully and heading off into the bush. As if in a daydream, they had gone on walking – walking into Africa. They had passed within ten yards of the food bank, without even noticing it. Dozens of fresh water containers, yams, bunches of bananas and piles of coconuts had been stacked near the path.

'Quick Clairie, catch them up and tell them to wait. Watch where you put your feet. They haven't got anything to eat. They mustn't go any further. I will stay here to make sure that the others take some of this.'

Clairie was a fast runner. Half an hour later, she came, puffing, back to him.

'Its all right Babba. They've found a tree and they are praying. They will stay there until you come.'

'A tree …?' There was no time to talk. Tom was at the top of the cliff path directing the Africans towards the food. He ran backwards and forwards between the cliff top and the food bank, helping to load people up with what they could carry. The water containers were awkward and needed two men to carry each of them. Out in the bay, another ship was lowering its sails. It would soon be dark. The people on board that vessel would have to wait until the next day. The last jolly-boat had landed and the last Africans were climbing the hill. Tom pointed them towards the food, then he and Clairie loaded themselves up with as much as they could carry and set off to follow. Just as Clairie had said, the Africans were sitting, lying or kneeling on the ground around a beautiful young cotton tree which stood by itself in the middle of a large grassy area. They were singing and praying. Tom saw the scene in the half light. The moon was rising. The smell of Africa, the sound of the crickets and cicadas, and the call of tree hyraxes stirred long-buried memories. Overcome by a sudden feeling of profound loss, he did not, at first, hear when Clairie spoke to him:

'Babba, are you all right?'

He regained his composure and put his arm around her. 'I am fine Clairie. We have come home. Isn't it beautiful?'

The next day storm-damaged sails were brought from the ships, and sailors were sent into the forest to cut branches to create shelters. The day after that, they were sent to cut roofing grass so that huts could be built. It was an opportunity for Clarkson to exert some control over the Council, who seemed disinclined to accept his authority. Tom thought them somewhat insolent.

The older Africans, who could remember how to build mud huts, instructed the others, many of whom had been born in America. Soon, they were all hard at work erecting the frames. The rains were coming. The grass had arrived, and the roofs went on first. Within the week, mud was in plentiful supply and Freetown became a township of mud huts, tents and canvas shelters, all built around a beautiful cotton tree.

John Clarkson was angry, and disappointed, to find that so little of what had been promised, had been accomplished. Faced with apparently insurmountable problems, his health, both mental and physical, began to suffer. The Council members were unfriendly and Clarkson was out of his depth. Every night when Tom went home to his cheerful family life, he thought of the poor young Governor. He worried that, with so little support, he must be wretchedly lonely. He had, anyway, been ill before they left Nova Scotia and the burden of responsibility was affecting his judgement, and causing Tom increasing anxiety. During one of his altercations with the Council, someone told the Governor that the Africans were demanding more self-regulation. Incensed, he turned on Tom and accused him of being a traitor. In fact, Tom had been avoiding the subject. He had decided not to mention it until Clarkson was under less pressure. However, Clarkson's behaviour towards him was so discourteous that, unusually for him, Tom lost his temper, and an angry quarrel developed. Clarkson, already furious with the Sierra Leone Company for lumbering him with a council, over which he had no control, now felt betrayed by Tom. He decided to return to England to confront the Company directors, face to face. He left Sierra Leone in a state of mental turmoil, which had not abated by the time he arrived in London. At the meeting, still seething with resentment, he reproached the directors so furiously, that, despite his brother, Thomas, being on the board, he was asked to resign. He refused and was fired. He was a passionate abolitionist who had been selected for his beliefs and his naval expertise, neither of which had equipped him for the burdensome task with which he had been faced. Although it was a sad end to

his career, he was engaged to a wealthy young woman, and, Tom comforted himself with the thought that, Clarkson's future would be happier and more fulfilling than his life in Sierra Leone.

After Clarkson's dismissal, William Dawes, a former officer in the Marines and a surveyor, in charge of land distribution, was appointed as Governor. He was a highly intelligent astronomer of outstanding ability. He was devoutly religious but so unyielding in his opinions that discussions became almost impossible. He immediately caused an upheaval by changing many of Clarkson's edicts. He infuriated the Africans by insisting that they move their already-planted allotments to a different area, and then he turned his attention away from land distribution, to build a fort on Thornton Hill. Because the fort required so much labour, the land clearance and distribution programme slowed down. Inevitably the people were angry and disappointed. In retaliation, they refused to obey his orders. He called a public meeting at which he threatened to return to England if they did not co-operate. They responded by shouting 'Go, go, go, go, go, go,' as they stamped their feet in unison.

Tom was frustrated at the prospect of another lot of land difficulties, but, at least, this time, he knew that the situation would eventually be resolved. Also, he agreed with Dawes that the colony needed more protection. Sierra Leone's coastal waters were protected by the Royal Navy who also guarded Bunce Island from French naval attacks. Bunce Island was a slaving post, owned by an English company. Every year, it dispatched thousands of slaves across the Atlantic. It was situated in the middle of the Rokei River on which most of Tom's people would depend for their fresh water. It's proximity concerned him.

Despite the obvious difficulties between Tom and Dawes, Tom had drawn up plans for the establishment of an African assembly which would give them partial self-regulation. It would be a democratic assembly in which the word 'democratic' related to both men and women. He was exhilarated to think that, in the not-too-distant future, they might reach the dawning of justice and equality for his people.

Other than the practical problems they were encountering, there were also intangible problems. The Nova Scotian Africans had returned to Africa, but could they return to being African in the context of their ancestors? His people worked well as a well-integrated and friendly community. Some had almost ceased to be tribally conscious. They were Christians, governed by English laws and English culture, and although some still clung to tribal traditions and beliefs, African culture was losing its influence. Tom reflected that the difficulties between him and Clarkson were partly caused by the fact that Clarkson believed that no culture, other than white culture, either could or, indeed, should, exist.

It was an attitude which offended those still torn between the two cultures, but with so many disparate tribes in West Africa, a compromise culture was inconceivable.

◂ ◂ 43 ▸ ▸

When they had first arrived in Sierra Leone, a doctor, sent by The Sierra Leone Company, had been on the Council. The doctor had become ill and the Company had arranged for a fully-equipped hospital ship to be sent from England. A married couple, respectively a doctor and a nurse, together with a schoolmaster came with the ship. They had all been paid for by a recently-established religious society. Tom went to interview them. He knew that their attitude towards him would mirror their attitude to their African patients. He wanted to know what that might be. At first he was not sure. They were polite but indicated that their plans were none of his business. He suggested to the doctor that he and his wife should train local girls as nurses and midwives. He thought it important for the colony's future. The doctor was perplexed. The Sierra Leone Company was English. What authority did this person of colour think that he had and why was he interfering? The doctor decided to ask the Governor to intervene. Dawes replied, rather testily:

'I am so sorry. I can't help you, I'm afraid. That man is King here. I am only the Governor.'

Tom had chosen six responsible and intelligent girls to be trained. The next day, the doctor asked to meet them. Having decided to give way gracefully, he had concluded that Tom's idea made sense. His wife would train them and it would transform his situation, especially if there was an epidemic. The doctor grew to respect Tom and they became friends. He was proposing to vaccinate the whole population against smallpox. Tom was pleased, remembering that the African Colonist troops under George Washington had been vaccinated, and had been far more resistant to smallpox than the unvaccinated British troops. Besides which he had heard that a tribe, not far from the Sierra Leone border, had recently contracted the disease.

The schoolmaster had come out, with the medical team, as a volunteer hospital orderly but now that the hospital had six nurses in training, he was free to go back to teaching Tom was relieved. The older children knew how to read, write and count, but there had been no one to teach mathematics to the boys. In England, the schoolmaster had taught Mathematics and Geography. He enjoyed teaching, but his main interest in life was football. A game, which, for centuries, had been so popular with young men, that it had often been outlawed in order to compel them to stop wasting time.

For a while, Tom had been acting as a part-time stone-mason, helping to build the public buildings. He had solved the Mathematics problem by taking the older boys with him to building sites. He made them calculate the cost of building materials, the quantities required, the pitch of the roof, the area of rooms, the length of the rafters, and anything else that he could think of. They were allowed to measure out where the walls were to be built, and they learnt to ensure that angles were accurate and that doors and windows fitted properly. As well as improving their mathematics they had learnt basic building skills. Soon he could leave them to level the ground and to dig the foundations of a building by themselves. It had worked well, but they needed more formal tuition. The last job they had done was to measure out and level a football pitch and put up the goal posts.

The schoolmaster spent his every spare moment constructing footballs. He organised the boys into teams and taught them the rules. It was not long before, not only every boy, (almost as soon as he could walk), but also every man in Freetown wanted to play. Tom persuaded Dawes, on the grounds that sport was thought to improve behaviour, to release more land for football pitches and, after only a few weeks, there were six adult teams, six boys' teams and three new pitches. The men had been working long hours to clear the land and to build the fort. Now, they worked with renewed vigour so that they could finish in time to play football in the afternoons. Tom soon understood why some of the English kings had been forced to prohibit football in order to raise a decent army. Young men had been playing football instead of practising archery. At the battle of Crécy, six thousand skilled bowmen fired forty-two thousand arrows a minute. Only three years later, the standard of archery had declined so drastically, that King Edward III had had to outlaw football. That, not being Tom's problem, he was delighted to see his people having fun. Rival teams had soon assembled their own spirited fan clubs and the game had become the perfect leisure-time activity for the whole community.

◂ ◂ 44 ▸ ▸

Tom still worried about Sally. She seemed to have less energy than when they were in Nova Scotia. If he asked her how she felt, she would reply:

'Don't you worry Tom, I am quite all right. I promise you. I am happy. The children are doing well, and we are in Africa. We are so lucky, aren't we?' and she would smile happily. Tom was relieved when she felt well enough to go back to teaching at the kindergarten, but the respite did not last.

The rains came, and with them came malaria and dysentry. Sally fell ill and within a week, she lay dying. Clairie and her brother were loved and cared for by the other mothers while Tom and one of the hospital nurses looked after Sally. Kindness and compassion were freely given. When he knew the end was coming, Tom collected his children to say goodbye to their mother. John was just six years old. Clairie was thirteen years old. She had inherited her father's strength of character. She knew what her mother would have asked her to do, and she did it. She did not make a fuss. She struggled with her own grief to care for her brother. After the funeral, Tom, devastated by their loss, stayed at home for two weeks cosseting his children. Friends brought comfort and provisions and, gradually, with their help, he established a routine which would enable him to go back to work, and Clairie and John to go back to school.

◂◂ **45** ▸▸

Freetown developed into a well-run township. The people were happy, well-fed and protected. Clairie had grown up and had married the son of a Pioneer. Tom had two grandchildren, Sarah and Joseph. John, his son, was shortly to be married. He and three of his friends had been allocated building plots next to the coconut plantation. Tom had spent the last month helping to build their houses. John's house was finished and furnished. It would make a good family home. Tom was pleased to think that the young people would be living next door to each other.

Tom still held daily assemblies on his verandah to help resolve his people's problems. Sometimes the verandah was crowded and sometimes only a few people came, but there had never been a day when no-one had come.

It was at this point in his life that Tom did, not the very most unwise thing that he had ever done – that had occurred on the day of his capture, but it was the second most unwise thing that he had ever done.

◂◂ **46** ▸▸

It was after the funeral of one of the Pioneers, when, at his evening assembly, a young mother asked him for a loan. Her child had a club foot. A surgeon had come from England and would be at the hospital only for another day. He had told the mother that he could operate to make the child able to walk, but it would be expensive. Tom had only a little money in the house, but the man who had died owed him some. He would be able to help the mother if he collected it. He excused himself from the evening assembly. The man had been one of his closest friends. Tom knew where he kept his money. He went, quite openly and took what he was owed. It never occurred to him that he was taking a risk or that anyone would think him capable of theft. He was mistaken. Either someone did think him capable of theft, or someone wanted to undermine his authority.

Back at the house, the young woman was waiting with Clairie. He gave her the money and some sixth sense made him say, 'Go now, and go quickly to the hospital. It is important. Clairie, please go with her.'

Scared by his tone of voice, the young woman picked up her child and she and Clairie left together. Tom stood wondering what had come over him to be so sure that the girl must leave immediately. Ten minutes later, a constable walked up the path. He was the son of a Pioneer and looked distinctly uncomfortable. 'I am sorry sir, Tom, sir, they say you taken some money.'

'It's all right, Hector. Who says?'

'I dunno, sir. The white constable came – told me to arrest you.'

He looked as if he was about to cry.

'Calm down, Hector. I did take the money. I was owed it. A little boy needed to see a doctor. I haven't still got it.'

'Oh, sir, what am I to do?'

'You must do your job, Hector. You have a wife and family. I will come with you to the court.' They walked along the street together and as they came to the court, Tom took hold of the manacles hanging from Hector's belt.

'Quick, put them on. It won't be the first time … and I won't resist arrest. I promise.' He grinned wryly.

They walked in to the court building, with Tom in manacles, and poor Hector trying to hold back his tears.

The white constable was standing there. 'Ah yes, you are charged with theft. Fill in this form. How will you plead?'

'Not guilty to theft. But I took the money.'

'So, you stole it.'

'No, I was owed it.'

'Well you will not prove that. The man was dead so that is theft.'

Tom said nothing. Finally, he was allowed home. He closed the door behind him and went into the kitchen to pour himself some water. It was still uncomfortably hot. He decided to sit outside. He was about to open the door when running footsteps crossed the verandah. He stepped back, as the door burst open to reveal John, his son, outraged and in tears. 'How could they? How could they? After all you have done …'

Tom put his arm round the furious young man.

'It's all right John. It will be all right.'

'No it won't. They can't do this. I will never forgive them. I am going to kill them if they put you in prison.'

'Calm down John, please, you must calm down. You must not talk like that. Brains not fists.' Ibrahim's words. John had reminded him of Carlos when he had discovered his father's involvement in slavery.

Clairie knew her father's integrity to be beyond reproach. She did not want to let him see how upset she was, so she stayed away the next day. Tom was perplexed. Was it possible that she thought he had committed a crime or was she unable to cope with her brother's rage? John refused to leave Tom's side, even dragging a pallet into Tom's bedroom so that he could sleep beside him. He was behaving like a guard dog. Tom smiled to himself at the thought of anyone trying to arrest him. With John in his present state of mind, he did not rate their chances very highly. That day as he sat waiting, Clairie arrived with her husband, her two children and John's fiancée, Jenny. At last John calmed down and was, eventually, persuaded by his sister, that his father was not in immediate danger. Tom liked Jenny. Her mother was the daughter of a Pioneer and her father was an Englishman who had arrived with the unit of ex-soldiers sent by the Sierra Leone Company as constables. John was calmer when Jenny was with him.

A month later, Tom was tried by a white judge and a black jury, all of them young and ambitious. He had arranged for Clairie to keep an eye on John, who had promised to stay away from the hearing. The court was packed with the older generation of Tom's people and more waited outside in the blazing sun. He told his story. The mother of the child was his main witness. The judge expressed scepticism, which caused an uneasy muttering in the court. The defence lawyer asked that the child be allowed in. The judge reluctantly agreed and the mother went to fetch him. She came, leading a happy-looking child by the hand. He could walk. One leg was still weaker than the other. He had a slight limp, but he was, otherwise, normal. The jurors had heard the court's reaction to the judge's scepticism. Now that they saw the child, they hesitated for a while, then accepted Tom's explanation. He was found guilty of theft because he had admitted taking money from a dead man. Finally, after pressure from the jurors, the judge gave way. Tom was told, in rather harsh terms, to repay the money together with two pounds to cover the cost of the case. He signed the relevant papers and went to leave the court. At the door stood the clerk. He looked at Tom and spoke with his lips barely moving. 'It's all paid, Tom, sir, every penny of it, man.' Their eyes met for a moment. Tom mouthed his thanks and walked out. But it was not so easy. He had been shamed and dishonoured. White people who would normally have greeted him, turned their backs. He even sensed a change in the younger Africans. The worst part was that his two children were deeply distressed, and, for the first time, he felt relieved that Sally was no longer alive. She had believed in him, she had loved him and she had been proud of him. He would go down in history (anyway, in English history) as a thief. That might have distressed her. But a child could walk … she would have rejoiced.

That evening was hot and humid. The short rains were due to begin. The sky was heavy with cloud. As usual, Tom sat on his verandah waiting for the evening assembly. Clairie and Sarah had come to be with him. Clairie had been more than distressed when Sarah had come home from school crying. A child had taunted her, singing, 'Your grandpa's a thie-ief.' Tom hated to see them so unhappy. He sat with Sarah on his knee and talked to her. He told her how proud he was of her, that she reminded him of her grandmother, and how much her grandmother would have loved her. He and Clairie had their own thoughts, and could do little to comfort each other.

As he sat, wondering whether his people would ever meet there again, Clairie suddenly let out a whoop. 'Oh my goodness, oh my goodness. Look at that!'

Instead of the usual trickle of Africans coming towards the house, a tidal wave of them had come round the corner, led by two of the ex-Pioneers. He stood and walked forward with Sarah still clutching his leg. The crowd stopped and the two leading men knelt and stretched their arms forward in tribal obeisance to their king. The sight of his people and the feel of Sarah's hand brought back a long-suppressed memory – the memory of a small boy holding the hem of a king's robe while the king, the child's father, spoke to his people. Tom waited. He raised his hand in welcome, and from the recesses of his mind came the words he had heard his father speak more than half a century earlier.

The two men stood up and the crowd, none of them young, spread out behind them. He heard Africa, the drums, the rhythm, the dancing, the singing. He heard, he saw and he understood. He signalled for them to stop. He was supposed to inform the authorities if they were planning to dance.

Minutes later, crashing thunder and lightning ripped through the sky, releasing a torrent of water. The rains had come. The dancing had stopped, and the crowd squeezed themselves on to the verandah. Clairie came out of the house, smiling through her tears as she greeted their guests. She carried a tray of sweetmeats. She had made them two days before, hoping that they would last a month. They were already half finished when John, who had just arrived, brought out the drinks. Long into the night they talked, telling and retelling legends from the past. Clairie took Sarah to bed in her old room before they began to talk of their lives as slaves, of the cruelty that they had endured, and the difficulties they had faced in Nova Scotia.

They were Tom's people. They knew what they owed him.

◂ ◂ **47** ▸ ▸

John's marriage was supposed to take place at the end of the rains, but the rains were lasting longer than usual. The heaviest rain of the day always came in the early afternoon. Neither John nor Jenny wanted to go on waiting. They asked the pastor if they could have the marriage ceremony in the morning. Tom hired the community hall. It would be crowded but at least it would be dry and the older generation would leave after the wedding feast allowing the young to dance and to enjoy themselves through the night.

Since the trial, John had become increasingly aggrieved about the way his father had been treated. Tom, with difficulty, persuaded him to invite those, against whom he had been inveighing, to his wedding. Tom was determined that John should be on good terms with the whole community. He was aware of his son's fiery temperament and worried that after he was gone, John might get himself into trouble. He was surprised but pleased when the white judge and his wife accepted the wedding invitation. John was not pleased. His father was resolute.

'John, It must have been a difficult decision for them. Now listen to me, John. As my son, you have a duty which is not negotiable, not now, not ever. It is to put the honour and welfare of our people and this community ahead of your own feelings.' For a whole minute, John stared at his father, the man that he admired above all others.

'All right Sir, I will do that, I promise.' The matter was settled.

The night before his wedding John stayed with Tom. He was gentle and considerate and wanted to talk about his mother and his parents' life before he was born. For Tom, who was not feeling well, it brought back memories and sleep eluded him. He tossed and turned and when, at last, he slept, he dreamt of Sally and of the twins. He missed them. He woke up, tired and headachey, and had just finished dressing, when a knock on the door announced the arrival of John's best man. He made coffee for them all, and the two young men went off to check that everything was ready in the church. Still feeling shaky, Tom drank another cup of coffee. He walked to the church to find John and his friends milling around in the aisle. John told him that Jenny's uncle was to sit beside the judge. It was a relief. Tom wanted the freedom to concentrate on his son. The congregation was seated. John and his best man stood at the altar steps. Tom and Clairie sat behind them. Tom felt increasingly unwell. Music. He turned to see the bride on her father's arm. A beautiful black bride on the arm of a white officer. Flashbacks. Memories. His eyes searched the aisle for the twins. Instead, he saw his grand-children, Sarah and Joseph standing behind Jenny. He felt dizzy and sick. It was John's wedding, not his. 'Get a grip. Keep your wits about you.' He admonished himself. His head was throbbing. There was a woman standing by the altar. Who was she? He stared. It was his mamma-woman. No, it couldn't be. He shut his eyes. Was he dying? 'Please God,' he prayed, 'not today, not here. Please, not today …' He looked again at the altar. His mamma-woman had gone. Jenny and her father had reached the altar steps. The service began. Tom's head ached. He had a fever and he desperately wanted to lie down. Self control. Rigid self control. The service over, he signed the register and went to the reception. Clairie guided him to one of the tables and told him to sit. She stood beside him. He made a speech to propose the health of the bride and groom. It was short – much shorter than he had intended. Throughout the reception, Clairie stood at his elbow, greeting the guests, but never moving away. After the feast, the older guests took their leave. Tom stood against the wall, as he wished them goodbye. Clairie put her arm through his. He leant against her and felt her push back. It was time to go.

He embraced his son and daughter-in-law. They were happy and excited about the party which was about to begin. Their friends had assembled a band of drums and banjos. African instruments. African music. He could hear the celebratory rhythm of the drums in the background. They would dance the night away.

'Don't you want to stay and dance with your children, Clairie?'

'No, Babba, you are not looking well. I will come with you.'

'I am all right. I just feel a bit hot.'

'I am coming with you Babba.'

He was swaying. Sweat was running down his face. Clairie pulled one of his arms over her shoulders and held his wrist to support him.

'Come on Babba, we are nearly there then you can rest.' She half-carried him to his chair on the verandah. She mixed cinchona powder into a cup of water and helped him to drink it. He undoubtedly had malaria. For a while he slumped, exhausted and semi-conscious as she fanned his face. When he came to, she helped him to his bed.

All that night she sat beside him sponging him with cold water to keep his temperature down. Sometimes he thrashed around muttering to himself, sometimes he fell asleep and sometimes he hallucinated, mistaking Clairie, either for her mother, or for someone called Nmula.

The next day Tom seemed better and was sleeping quietly. Clairie was relieved. Her husband and children called in. Sarah wanted to stay with her grandfather. Joseph wanted to play with Tom's old football. He and his father went out to play, leaving Sarah and Clairie with Tom, who had just woken up. Clairie asked him if he was hungry. He answered:

'Yes, Clairie, I am rather. Could I have a scrambled egg please?'

'Of course you can, Babba, I won't be long.'

She turned to Sarah.

'Sarah, stay with Grandfather while I get some eggs for his tea. Your babba is outside playing with Joseph. Call him if you need him. I won't be very long.' Sarah loved her grandfather and he loved her. She said 'Don't worry Mamma, I will look after him, I promise.' Tom smiled and closed his eyes.

Sarah did not know that he was dying. She sat beside him, fanning his forehead, and singing the songs that he had taught her. Tom felt his life force ebbing slowly away. It was time to send the child to her mother.

'You are a good girl Sarah. Thank you for looking after me, darling. Go now and kiss your mamma for me.' His voice was faint. She stood up to leave. A tall elderly man stood in the door way. Who was he? Sarah thought that he looked different. She hesitated.

The stranger smiled.

'I will look after him.' he said, and having waited until she went out, he crossed to Tom's bed and knelt beside it.

'Tom?'

Tom caught his breath. It was the voice of an old man but, into his mind, flashed the face of a teenage boy. Joy and happiness filled his heart as he struggled to open his eyes. The voice spoke again:

'Oh, Tom …'

With failing strength Tom gripped the hand that held his.

'Carlos, … At last, Don't cry, man. Don't cry.' He fell back, speaking quietly. Carlos leant forward 'Pater Noster Qui Es In Caelis;' Together, they prayed 'Sanctificetur Nomen Tuum; Adveniat Regnum Tuum; Fiat Voluntas Tua … The grip on Carlos's hand loosened as Tom's voice trailed off.

The funeral took place the following day. Hundreds of people from both communities were there. The rain had stopped. It was a hot day and the service was held outside. Carlos gave the address. He began by saying:

'I am the son of a slaver. Through perverse good fortune, the slave trade brought Tom to my father's fort. He became not only my childhood companion, but my brother in all but blood. He changed my life and, because of him, I had a wonderful childhood. Today, fifty years later, he has changed your lives, and because of him, you will, I hope, have a wonderful future. As boys, we

planned to put an end to the slave trade. That didn't quite work out. We were captured and forcibly separated …'

That night Carlos stayed with Tom's family and close friends. They huddled, tearfully, together in Tom's house. His children were comforted by Carlos's presence, and his connection to Tom's past, about which he had never spoken. His children wanted to know everything that Carlos could tell them. He told them about Tom's mamma-woman, about his parents, about Ibrahim, about the servants and about their minders and their guards. He described the fort, the beach, the adventure days, the fishing, swimming on the reef, the traders, the camels, and the dancing in the men's courtyard. Clairie and John questioned him endlessly. He ended by saying: 'It was our own fault that we were captured by the white slavers …'

It was nearly dawn before finally they fell asleep. When they awoke, Carlos had gone.

TOM PETERS

BIRTH 1738 (not verifiable)

ENSLAVEMENT 1750s

(DUNMORE PROCLAMATION 1775)

ENLISTMENT IN BRITISH ARMY 1776

(PHILLIPSBURG PROCLAMATION 1779)

ARRIVED IN NOVA SCOTIA 1783

LONDON 1791

SIERRA LEONE 1792

DEATH 1792

FIGURES OF HISTORICAL INTEREST

GENERAL SIR HENRY CLINTON (1730–1795)
British Commander-in-Chief, American Revolutionary War

JOHN CLARKSON (1764–1828)
First Governor of Sierra Leone (July to September 1792)

GRANVILLE SHARP (1735–1813)
Slave Trade Abolitionist

WILLIAM DAWES (1762–1836)
Governor of Sierra Leone 1792–1794
and subsequently twice more after that

JOHN PARR
Governor of Nova Scotia

SIR GUY CARLETON
Commander-in-Chief of British forces in North America from 1782
and Governor General of the Canadas from 1786.

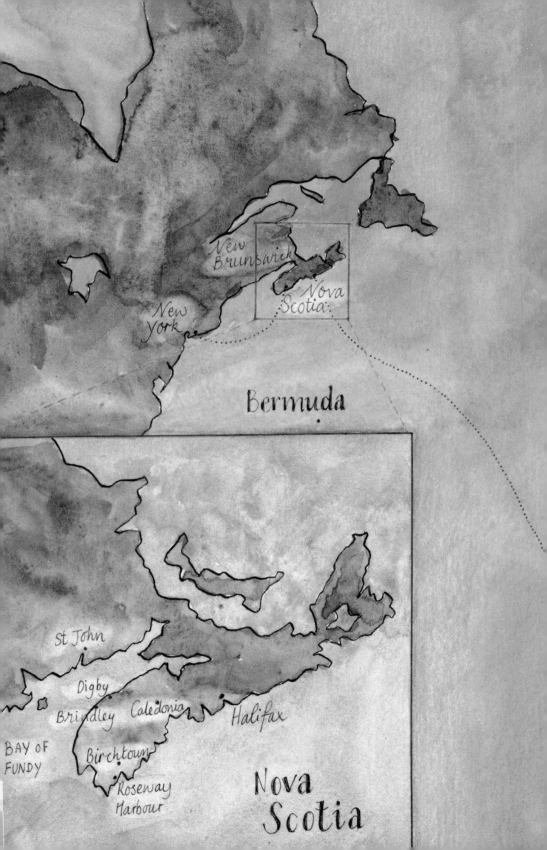